The BOOK of FORMATION

The BOOK of FORMATION

A NOVEL

Ross Simonini

The BOOK
of
FORMATION

First Melville House Printing: November 2017

Melville House Publishing
46 John Street
Brooklyn, NY 11201

and

8 Blackstock Mews
Islington
London N4 2BT

mhpbooks.com
facebook.com/mhpbooks
@melvillehouse

ISBN: 978-1-61219-668-8

Printed in the United States of America

10 9 8 7 6 5 4 3 2 1

A catalog record for this book is available
from the Library of Congress

The highest bliss on earth shall be

The joys of personality!

—GOETHE

Preface

For two decades I interviewed the man who helped us to stop being ourselves and become who we want to be. I was fortunate enough to know him well and in many forms: as a celebrity, hermit, mentor, target of media slander, miracle worker, director of a multimillion-dollar media empire, and uncultured teenage fledgling, which is how I first met him on a winter morning in Los Angeles.

Most people never knew Masha Isle. They didn't meet the boy who uttered every word with perfect ignorance. They met someone else: the fully formed adult, master of the personality arts—worldly, seasoned, glowing from televisions and presiding over his audiences like a natural-born leader.

This book is my attempt to reintroduce the world to Isle. For those who know him through gossip and tabloids, here is a chance to meet him directly, without the pesky buzz of opinion. For devotees of his show, these talks reveal the icon as he was offstage, out of his host position. For those who haven't known Isle at all—the next generations—I hope this book serves as an authentic introduction.

Of course, to be properly introduced to the boy, you must first meet the mother. Anyone who lived through those premillennial years knew the name Mayah long before the arrival of her boy successor, and this, too, is how I met the Isles, in the final days of 1994.

Ah, the '90s—the moment I discovered I could work on myself. *Actualize*, as the saying then went. A decade of looking through the mirror. Self-transformation certainly wasn't a new concept, but to experience it then, when it was finally accepted into pop culture—that felt historic. Here was a new way to believe—no more years of studying the dreary history of religion. By then, all you needed was pure human potential.

When these talks began, *Mayah!* was in its eighth nationally syndicated season, the clear frontrunner among a wave of talk shows. These were collectively known as "PM" or "personality movement." Likewise, Mayah's growing mass of admirers referred to themselves as "personality movers" (or simply "movers") and included a cast of celebrities whose endorsements lifted her to the most rarified peak of the American media landscape.

I admit, at this time in my life, I only knew the vague contours of PM. I had the same basic knowledge as any half-aware U.S. citizen. I could recite a bit of the movement's jargon, but I didn't really understand it, and I'd seen a few episodes of the show, mostly to study Mayah's dynamic interviews with guests. I'd heard people making claims of radical transformations, shedding bad habits, eradicating unwanted opinions, but to me it all sounded like overwrought psychoanalysis.

There were a slew of other hosts—Dr. Mark Todd, Tello Jeffers, Vicki Shore, Donel—and they all carved out their individual niches and interpretations of "p," which, as best as I could understand, was some kind of energy substance at the root of our identities. But mostly, like everyone else, my attention was fixed on Mayah, who seemed to draw her energy out of an endless well of charm from which we all wanted to drink.

She was pervasive—on every red carpet, her arm around every head in show business. Within a few years, I watched as the media's fascination with Mayah's celebrity blossomed into a certainty that this woman would progress our culture toward enlightenment. The majority had crossed a threshold, from skepticism to belief. Every food she ate, ensemble she wore, suggestion she made—the press received it all as wisdom.

Unlike most celebrities, Mayah asked for a kind of attention that felt productive. We could all see how she was developing an important new role for society. And yet, as much as we loved her, it was obvious that the system of thought behind her words wasn't going to catch on. Her vigilance was endearing, and her sermons on the show were uplifting, but ultimately, all the talk about "p" seemed just too opaque for popular consciousness. The expanse of PM wasn't suited for six-hundred-word articles, so journalists usually glossed over it in a clause or two. You'd hear people throw the terms back and forth—"Inhale P. Exhale Personality."—to show off their knowledge of pop trivia, but rarely did anyone dive beneath the movement's reputation as the newest way to make yourself over. PM was everywhere, yes, but no one was really paying attention, which is how one of the great ideas of the late twentieth century developed, hidden in plain sight.

For me, the whole thing floated by like a ship off the coast—impressive, but of no personal concern. I wasn't the target audience and I had no stake in the game, which was exactly how I liked to observe the drift of fads. For a journalist, this was the preferred position: cool neutrality. The idea was to purge yourself of opinion and become a blank slate on which to deliver the truth. Culture trusted you, and the way to honor that trust was to escape your own bias.

I spent years cultivating this attitude. I'd molded my voice to the shape of highbrow journals. I interviewed intellectuals on theory, politicians on policy, and moguls on ethics. Pop culture, on the other hand, was an alien landscape to me.

All this changed in 1994, when I accepted an uncharacteristically light assignment to profile Mayah. An editor at a now-defunct glossy magazine called me and mentioned the idea. She thought it might be provocative to put a heady writer such as myself on a sugary story like this. In fact, she'd already pitched my name to Mayah's publicist and received an encouraging response.

I accepted because it seemed like the right kind of challenge, and because the minor accolades of small academic publications were starting to feel meager. I wanted to know what it would feel like to write something for the general reader. I also knew enough about Mayah to know that she granted interviews only rarely. She relished making grand ideological proclamations about her privacy, and irately rebuffing the paparazzi. My hope was to be the first interviewer to debate her deeply, to get her on the defensive and coax something unexpected from her. Why she agreed to speak with *me*, I could not say, but I recognized the opportunity and I took it.

The plan was to fly to Los Angeles and chronicle the rising queen of television in six thousand zeitgeisty words. I shadowed Mayah for five days and I attended two live tapings of the show. Each week, *Mayah!* focused on a single "guest" making a "turn" from one personality to a new one. Shows featured ongoing interviews with the guest's family and friends, lectures that related the guest's progress, plus film clips of offstage treatments. Every so often, Mayah would bring one of her favorite transformational writers on the show to help tease out the nuances of the guest's situation.

That particular week's guest, Julie B., came from the state of Idaho, was addicted to aerosol, and had a penchant for verbally abusive partners, all of whom had their own idiosyncratic addictions. She blamed her personality.

My first show was on a Thursday, a day known for being boisterous and unpredictable due to the onstage "p-form lessons." I'd been keeping up with the show to prepare for the article, but I was still a little shocked by the kinds of primal-looking fits that took place that afternoon. Julie B. flailed around the stage for twenty minutes while the house band clapped and stomped. Finally, she exhausted herself, collapsed onto the bed, and became docile enough to allow Mayah to wag her limbs and "rub out that stale p."

For the second taping, Julie B. was in treatment backstage, and we watched a short surveillance video of her as she lay unconscious, getting massaged with white oil. Then Mayah held a forty-minute "intensive cry." Photographs from Julie's childhood projected above us, alternately cute and heartbreaking, accompanied by cooing gospel music. Mayah commented on each image, telling little anecdotes to illuminate Julie's tendencies toward self-destructive behaviors, until, one by one, the audience joined in for the sob. This, Mayah explained, was a "cleansing ritual," both for the audience and Julie, and though I didn't personally experience any tears, it seemed undeniable that the people around me were moved.

Over the next few days, I interviewed the show's staff and visited the homes of a few of the show's vocal supporters, including the actress Billie Gaines, who told me that Mayah had "rearranged" her life with just a few meetings. However, when I asked for a deeper description of the meetings, Gaines declined, saying that she had only "a few nooks of discretion in her life," and her personality work was one of them.

Most importantly, I got some face time with Mayah. However, while her show depicts an earnest and forthcoming extrovert, her dealings with the press are consistently reserved, reluctant, and occasionally spiteful. In my few brief interviews with her, Mayah proved to be an expert in the evasive remark. Though she was never directly rude to me, I couldn't seem to get past the series of verbal games she'd placed between us. She managed to avoid making any clear, direct statements or revealing any factual information about herself. She'd respond to a question with an unrelated answer and would laugh in moments that seemed entirely inappropriate. Each reply felt like a small provocation to my dialogic skills, and so I pushed on competitively, trying to speak to her on her own elusive terms.

For the longest of these talks, Mayah and I met in an intimate, conical room walled almost entirely in mirrors. She called it the "rec room," which I later learned was an abbreviation of "recovery room," a place where guests come after they've taken a turn. For me, the room was a nightmare. My reflection kept peering at me from over both of Mayah's shoulders, bobbing in my peripheral vision like a persistent sprite. It was all I could do to keep my eyes on her. She, of course, rolled along comfortably, unaffected by the reflections, her face sculpted into an impermeable Mona Lisa smile.

Again, I asked my questions, but each one was casually volleyed back as a new question, and pretty soon, I started to answer them. She had me rambling about my life, my career, and my recent personal failures. If I'm honest, I was too flattered by her interest not to give thoughtful responses. Even when I tried to turn the table, to segue into the topics I'd prepared in my notes, she'd take me down another conversational alley and watch as I struggled to find my way out of it.

I managed to disclose the place and time of my birth, the story of how I began professionally interviewing, the contempt I had for a certain sweaty-necked contingent of Mayah's fans, and, finally, my candid reasons for accepting the assignment. My interviews were exercises in compassion, I told her, and this piece was a way for me to try and understand a person who was utterly alien to me. I went on to freely describe my pre-interview protocol, where I close my eyes, imagine the interviewee sitting across from me, and anticipate the first few minutes of the exchange. Mayah seemed to love all of this, hooting and clapping, encouraging me to tell her everything.

Had she slipped me a pill? Something to loosen my tongue? I couldn't believe myself, willfully saying these things to a subject. I had thought that after interviewing so many significant cultural figures I had developed some kind of an immunity to the inflated ego. But on that day, when Mayah showed her curiosity toward me, I found myself under her spell, weak-kneed, vulnerable. She showed me the glaring truth: I want attention. Maybe not worldwide fame, maybe not all the time, but I want to be noticed, just like everyone else does.

This embarrassment might have been the end of my relationship with the Isle family, but the next morning, after eating three croissants to make myself feel better, I got a call from Mayah's assistant, Toni, asking if I'd be interested in speaking to "Mayah's boy" the next day.

I was, of course, shocked. It was only a few hours before I was leaving to catch my flight home, and after my botched interview experience with Mayah, this unsolicited invitation to speak with her immediate family member seemed like the most unlikely offer I could imagine receiving.

So I spent a solid hour perched on the edge of my hotel bed, semiparalytic, wondering why Mayah would ask this, now, of me. What had gone right the day before? I did my typical yay-nay rumination, but eventually accepted, for the sake of the piece. The assistant gave me an address and asked me to arrive the following morning at 7:00 a.m., the moment when the following interviews begin.

I know the early conversations in this book will elicit mixed responses. Readers will interpret Masha's stories of his youth as unfortunate—the disadvantaged, helpless child preyed upon by adults. Others will see him as a spoiled brat who was bequeathed the golden crown of fame. But to see him either way will only transform every phrase he utters into evidence of your own narrow perspective. You will simplify a man who was never simple, and who was never anyone's prey.

You can be sure that whoever you are, Masha comes from a different culture than you. A culture of one, you could say. So give him the same courtesy you'd give a foreigner, someone raised in a place you've never been, with a lifestyle you will never understand. I have no interest in swaying your opinions. See Masha how you want—victim or prince—but also acknowledge that the person in these pages is free of your cultural toxins, and has been absolved from the social expectations into which all of us were involuntarily born.

The Book of Formation

Ross Simonini

I.

December 1994

LOS ANGELES, CA

Before Masha, I supported every interview I conducted with hours of careful research. I read as many conversations with my subjects as were available to the public. I familiarized myself with the tenor of their speech. I learned the topics they dodged and the ones that triggered negative reactions. I paid special attention to their underdiscussed passions, the avocations they'd only mentioned in passing, and would bring them up at the ideal moment in the conversation, usually to pleasant surprise: "So how long have you been collecting Flemish portraiture?" Most importantly, I'd get a sense of the questions that had been asked of the subject too many times before, the ones that elicited the kinds of rote responses nobody ever wants to hear. Even if I ignored all this research during the main performance (which is how I always thought of my interviews), the knowledge was always valuable.

For my interview with Masha, however, preparation was impossible. Not that I didn't try. Even in the two hours I had to research, I made a few hurried attempts. I called my pop-savvy friends, but they'd never heard of him. I leafed through the folder of press I'd brought for the Mayah interview—no mention of any children. Finally, I explored the liquor store beneath my hotel and discovered three short articles about Mayah's "immigrant" son, all of which I found in tabloid magazines. These gave me a small foothold, but were of no significant help. They all recycled the same anecdote, and each was basically a three-hundred-word elaboration of the headline "Mayah's Adopted Teenage Boy!" All were accompanied by the same bleary photo of Mayah ducking into a black car on Santa Monica Boulevard. Beside her, you could just barely see a figure wearing sunglasses, a black cap, and what looked like a white hotel bathrobe. When I finished reading these, I had no more time left to research and in a funny way, I was relieved. The impossibility of planning felt like a small liberation. Nothing was expected of me.

As I approached the Isle compound from Beverly Glen Boulevard, only the turret on the main house's gabled roof was visible. But then, once off the main road, I began to see a compound of buildings, surrounded by a thicket of laurels and oaks. A security guard greeted me at the gate and pointed me toward a road that snaked down a hill past the main house and ended at a small Spanish cottage.

I parked and saw a young person—maybe sixteen years old—leaning in the doorway, observing me with such a dispassionate expression that I wondered whether I had driven to the right house. The smooth face could be of either gender, and the person's stance, the angle and weight of it, seemed equally anomalous. I smiled, a little hesitantly, and they waved me over. This was Masha.

As I approached, his physical beauty confused me, as if I were looking at a photo of a person, seeing him from a single fixed perspective. His skin looked airbrushed, undisturbed by the elements. His hair swayed in a hypnotic dance with the wind. From his neck hung a thin chain with a name tag, and I could see the beginnings of what looked like a tattoo emerging from the cuff of his sleeve. I reached for a handshake but he refused with a kind of nonchalance that diffused the insult of it.

We talked for an hour in the cottage, which was entirely unfurnished except for the simple, handcrafted wooden table and chairs where we sat. I placed the whirring microcassette recorder directly in front of him and made sure he was paying full attention as I clicked it on. I always like both parties to be willfully engaged in the whole process. As I see it, this is the subject's conversation as much as it is mine.

I began with a couple of questions I'd sketched out in my notebook, but within a few exchanges, I abandoned them entirely. As we spoke, Masha snacked from a bowl of soaked acorns that I initially mistook to be decorative.

* * *

INTERVIEWER: I'm not sure if you know why I'm here today, but, just to explain, I'm writing about Mayah and was hoping to ask a few questions about your relationship with her. Nothing tricky. You can answer however you like. And if you don't want to answer a question, of course that's fine too.

MASHA ISLE: *[chewing]*

I: OK, so to start, how long have you been living here?

MI: I don't live in here.

I: No, I meant *here*, on the property, with your mother.

MI: She's not my mother. She just calls herself that. To explain us to people.

I: I'm sorry, your adoptive mother.

MI: No, no. She's more than that. She's my doctor.

I: Oh . . . But you do live here with her, right?

MI: Yeah.

I: Does she give you some kind of treatment?

MI: Yeah.

I: And how's that go? You just talk about yourself with her? Like on the show?

MI: I don't know.

I: Her show, I mean.

MI: I know what you mean. I haven't seen it.

I: Really? Ever? How's that—

MI: Never. It's not healthy for me to see her like that, in such a little box, so far away. She thinks it'll confuse me, which is true. I didn't know she had a show till I came out here. How would I even see it?

I: What do you mean? It's on TV. It plays every day.

MI: *[shrugs]* Yeah, I don't know. I don't watch any of that. I'm not supposed to.

I: So Mayah doesn't let you watch *any* television?

MI: She doesn't command me. She just explains it till it makes sense.

I: It's funny, at this point I just assume everyone has seen the show.

MI: Not where I'm from.

I: And where's that?

MI: *[points]*

I: What's that? North?

MI: *[chews]*

I: Or maybe you could say what town? Unless you'd rather not.

MI: No town. Just our house. Just me and my family.

I: So you and your parents . . . any siblings?

MI: Just Mimo and Polpy and this sack of p right here. *[points to himself]*

I: OK. And so how'd you meet Mayah?

MI: Oh, I've known her forever.

I: Your whole life?

MI: Even before. *[laughs] Way* before.

I: As your doctor.

MI: Always, yes.

I: To be honest, I didn't know she was a doctor. What kind

of doctor are we talking about here? Like a therapist or—

MI: Everything. Like regular. Anything I need.

I: Hm. So when's the first time you met her for treatment?

MI: When I first needed it. After Mimo's turn. Before that, I didn't even have any p in me so it didn't matter.

I: You didn't have p?

MI: Some, some. But not *real* p yet. Not adult p. I was still just tugging along.

I: And how old were you then?

MI: I don't know. Barely able to move. Probably same as when you first went to the doctor for p.

I: I don't think I did that. I'm not—I don't follow Mayah's program or anything, if that's what you mean. I apologize if I'm not picking up on the lingo.

MI: *[laughs]* No, it's fine, it's OK.

I: So you were learning to move—

MI: Oh yeah, all I did was flop around. I couldn't even stand. What a tug! Polpy'd ask me to hold a pose for the day and I couldn't even do it. I'd be as still as I could, but the only thing I'd ever think about was how much I hated him for telling me what to do. Even though he just wanted to make me better at loving.

I: At loving?

MI: Oh yes. But all I cared about was my knees and being bored.

I: And you're saying this is how you learned how to stand. Your father taught you?

MI: Yeah.

I: And how did he do that?

MI: Oh, he'd get my bones in the right position. He'd give little taps on my p parts or feel if I was shaking anywhere. He'd get me up and posed until he couldn't see any problems and I'd hold it and he'd sit back and watch me until everything looked perfect. And when I was done we'd snack on mashed corms with hot honey. Then we'd do another.

I: Another pose?

MI: Yeah.

I: So this is like, what—two or three years old? I'm just trying to get a sense of what size you were, learning to stand.

MI: Here. *[raises hand to his sternum]*

I: Oh, so older then . . . Eleven? Twelve?

MI: *[yawns]*

I: But, so then it wasn't like you *couldn't* stand. It was more—

MI: Yeah, I couldn't do it.

I: Were you being rehabilitated or trained or—I'm sorry if I'm missing something here . . .

MI: No, it was just something I got worse at the older I got. Mimo was always saying I put too much p in my pose. Such as when I was cooking, I'd hang over the pot like a worm while I stirred the soup. And she'd be in the chair across the room pointing out my parts. "Pose, Mashy! I can see your little p chirping from over here."

I: "Stand up straight" kind of thing?

MI: Never straight. No, no. Polpy rubbed all straightness out. He wanted me to feel the p streaming through my navel and buttom and everywhere. And he'd just watch and sew, watch and sew, till I got it right.

I: But what was he looking for?

MI: *[shakes his head]* Watch Mayah do it. She *knows* how to stand. She's posing all day long. She's not just propped up, hoping she won't fall over—which, that's how it was with me. Mayah *loves* to stand. I didn't. A puff of wind could've pushed me over. But I didn't care. I just wanted to be at the creek, building little dams. Sneaking round the house. Tug stuff.

I: And these exercises, the way you describe them, it sounds like they hurt.

MI: Yeah, but not *real* pain. Just fake pain I made up. I'd lie in bed all night and my legs would twitch and twitch.

I: That sounds pretty real to me.

MI: No, no. It was my game. I couldn't even sleep, so I'd pretend I was in pain and all night I'd listen to Polpy honking down the hallway. *[makes a snoring sound]* But it was also one of my favorite things to do. Being awake like that. Listening to the honks.

Because I knew *everything* that was happening. I could hear any sound. Even when Mimo sneaked out of bed and out of her room and into Puppy Paws. The honking was too great for both of us to sleep through.

I: What's Puppy Paws?

MI: Her own little den. Mimo painted it as if baby foxes had skipped across the walls because she was once a fox and it was good for her to be surrounded by paws so she could remember her past life. And my room was always on the other side of Puppy Paws so I could hear every little sound she made, even such as when she picked up an ashtray and tapped it with her pipe. I could even hear that. Or when she tippy-toed to the far side of the room to write about me. Or when she went to the bath to mix up paste for morning face work. I could listen all night without anyone knowing.

I: And you did this every night?

MI: *But* the problem was Polpy's honking was sometimes so good I couldn't hear Mimo through the wall. Sometimes she'd go downstairs or walk through the hallway and she'd be too far away, which I didn't like because I'd get bored. I hated when I couldn't know what was going on. So I got out of bed and sneaked all night like a wood rat, which is how I learned that sneaking is the greatest of all games.

I: Did—

MI: And then after that all I ever did was think about how to get sneakier. I'd stuff snacks around the house in hiding spots so I could be nothing but a shadow behind the ferns, eating berries all night. Or I could fold myself into a wicker basket perfectly. Or squat behind the curtains like a frog.

I: And what was your mother doing when you watched?

MI: Smoking. Or she'd light candles and fill her pipe and hum. And she wrote in her Masha Journal, where she put everything that ever happened to me. A single day would be more words than I'd ever spoken in my life.

I: Was—

MI: But the problem was that I was still missing things, which I hated. I didn't have enough good spots to see *everything*. Such as if she wanted to lie on the floor and cry, I couldn't see her.

I: From your spot.

MI: So what I started doing was—I said to myself, "How could I go from this spot here where I'm sitting, to that spot over there *[points at the wall across the room]* without being seen?" Without anything seeing me. With you sitting right there—how could I do that?

I: Uh, you couldn't, right? There's nowhere to hide. It's just open space.

MI: But! But! What if I had no body? What if I was pure p? Then it would be different, right?

I: You know, I don't mean to cut you off but if we could get back to Mayah—I'm just not sure how much time we have left, and you were telling me before about meeting her . . .

MI: That's what I'm saying.

I: Oh.

MI: I thought that's what we were talking about.

I: Sorry. It is, I guess. I just wasn't sure if—

MI: Yeah.

I: OK, sure, then back to what you were saying. Moving across the room without being seen—is this a riddle?

MI: So what I was about to say is, I'd go down to the creek and practice getting better at being a ghost. I'd take off my sandals and I'd pump my feet up and down until all the p was pointed at the ground, until I could feel each little stone moving between my toes, as if I was walking on living bugs and I didn't want to hurt them. And if I was doing good, I'd move from one side of the creek to the other without making even one sound on one pebble. Like a deer. I always wanted to be a deer. Since I was a baby. *[walks his hands nimbly across the table]* How funny is it to see a deer move like that. Right? But it's true too.

I: You—

MI: I'd follow them everywhere. All my life. But they'd always hear me and fly away. I could sneak behind them forever, but only if they let me do it, which they never did. The most sensitive animal in the forest. My favorite friend.

I: Sounds kind of lonely. Were there other kids around?

MI: Just Polpy and Mimo who were pure adults. But deer can be like kids.

I: Well—

MI: How I loved to change myself into a deer! Every day, I'd do it, even though I could never truly sneak on them. But I *could* sneak up on Mimo. Because I knew her moves. That was the greatest difference between Mimo and deer. Such as when she'd get up from her chair I could rise out from the back *[lifts his hands up off the table]* and move with her like I was her own body.

I: Behind her?

MI: If she went this way, I went this way. If she bent down, I bent down.

I: Following her.

MI: Stand up. I'll show you.

I: *[stands]*

MI: I don't know your specific moves yet, but it would be like this . . . *[positions himself behind I]* Now just go round the room like regular.

I: *[reaches for a glass of water, leans back in chair, stands up]*

MI: Now look for me. Find me.

I: *[looks over both shoulders, looks between his legs]* Yeah, yeah. That's fun. You're not there. You're a ghost.

MI: You see?

I: *[fakes left, looks right]* Ha. That's pretty good. Ninja-like.

MI: *[sitting back down]* And I can't even do it right anymore. I used to be like nothing. Just a smell. That's all I could be. And what if you didn't even know I was here? You wouldn't even know. I could float behind you forever. That's how it was with Mimo. I could follow her perfectly. Even though I was a child, I could act totally adult if I wanted to.

I: So how long did this go on for, following your mother around in the middle of the night?

MI: Oh, forever.

I: You like that word.

MI: But at a certain point it stopped, too. Mimo caught me sneaking, and everything was ruined and I had to just stay in bed for the rest of my life and twitch my knees and pretend to sleep. And that's when I first started hating when people know things.

I: Because she found you out.

MI: She didn't tell me that she knew, but she stopped moving like a person who is truly alone. She was *letting* me play my game, which I hated. She and Polpy always did that. They'd always say: *[in monotone voice]* "You're in control here, Mashy. You can ask us to do whatever you want."

I: When did they say this?

MI: It was just a boring game we played. Mimo would say, "Tell me what to do." And I said, "Put your toes in your mouth," and she'd do it, and then I'd say, "Put some of the raccoon's backstory into a pot and cook it," and she'd do it!

I: Backstory. *[laughs]* I like that.

MI: We did this with Polpy, too, but he was bad at it. He always had to *know* everything.

I: Sounds like a kid's dream, that kind of role reversal.

MI: No, just boring. I preferred being sneaky.

I: But you couldn't do that anymore?

MI: Oh, there were still times to be sneaky, especially when Mimo's friends came over. I could sneak on them too. But it just wasn't as fun.

I: Who were they?

MI: Just her best friends. They came to the house and I hated them, of course. I was always hating new people because Mimo changed every time they came over. She'd paint her eyes like a mole and then acted like nothing mattered. She'd just smile when her friends were there, even if I was biting her on the arm and rolling my head down the stairs, which I loved to do in front of the friends. And then she'd be in the basement all night with them and they'd be screaming and in the morning she'd come upstairs and her face would look terrible to me. It was always like that. Her friends ruined everything.

I: What were they doing in the basement?

MI: I wasn't allowed to know because they loved secrets. I was always to be in my room and they were always to be downstairs with the door closed and locked, singing and having true fun. Polpy was boiling up a pot of smelly trees in the kitchen, which was only for them to drink, and not me. And if

Polpy caught me sneaking, then I'd have to drink his famous vinegar drops to make me sleep.

I: So, if you had to guess, what do you think they were doing down there—the women?

MI: Oh, drinking tea, talking games, smoking, giving rubs. Adult lady stuff. But all I ever got to see were dark heads bobbing up and down the driveway, in and out of the basement. Except on one night—which is what I was telling you about.

I: When?

MI: When I saw lights in the yard and I sneaked to the window and the women were near a fire in the pit and they were pulling off their hair and whipping it onto the coals.

I: Their hair?

MI: Oh yeah. They would dance up to the fire, reach up like this *[raises his arm in a balletic arc]* and remove their hair. And then they'd sing and fling it into the pit.

I: Like a single hair?

MI: No, all of it. All of the hair they ever wore.

I: Like wigs?

MI: And underneath they had no real hair at all. Even Mimo. She put her big braid of tree-colored hair in the fire and she stuck her big nose over the smoke and *breathed* it into her eyes.

I: Was Mayah there?

MI: Of course!

I: I feel like she's been pretty vocal about her baldness, right? That gleaming head is part of what makes her so iconic. The way she yanks off the hairpiece throughout the show and cackles.

MI: And all of them were like that. Running around. Patting their heads. All their little hills and buttoms flapping. *[claps]*

I: They were naked?

MI: Of course! But I couldn't see them very close, which I hated.

I: I'm learning that about you.

MI: And so I went around the back of the house by the biggest hedge so I could *really* see them cooking their hair. And some of them were crying into the stew too. But not regular tears. More like the kind of crying you *have* to do because of your eyes getting hot from smoke. *[juts head forward, mimes crying]* And they were also spooning the stew on their legs and heads . . .

I: Had you ever seen this before?

MI: No, no. I'd been sleeping through this for years. What a night to be missing! All of the ladies covered in stew and I couldn't tell any of them apart. Fat round shadows everywhere, singing to the sky. *[sings] "Not you! Not you! Not me! Not him or her or you or me!"* You know that one?

I: Uh.

MI: Mayah always sings it.

I: I don't think I do.

MI: Yeah, they sang it with the mud stew on. You know it. *[hums tune again]*

I: I don't.

MI: And they all laughed Mayah's laugh. *[makes a "huff huff huff" sound]*

I: She does have a distinctive laugh.

MI: Yes, the laugh's got so much p in it. You've got to be careful. You've got to be able to really move it. Like, for my own laugh, if I can get it right here *[grips his throat]* and move it up *[brings hand in front of his mouth]* and also move it down *[sweeps hands down to stomach in a fist]* then I can work it around a little *[slides hand counterclockwise over torso]* and then I can pass it to you, which is the fun part.

I: How do you pass it to me?

MI: You make the same laugh.

I: I imitate you?

MI: Mm hm. And that's how Mimo did it that night. I watched

her. She passed it around the group until someone pitched with her.

I: Can you slow down a second? I'm not sure I'm getting this.

MI: It's easy. First there are different laughs from all the different ladies. Each one has her own laugh, and every p is loud, all at once. But then, when all the ladies push their p together, their laughs become the same.

I: So they're all laughing at once and it sounds like one person.

MI: Yes! And what a thing to have in your ears! All women laughing perfectly together. And then, if they do very good, it gets quiet and if they pitch just perfect you can't even hear it anymore.

I: But they are still laughing.

MI: But that doesn't happen unless it's so good.

I: It, like, cancels itself out? Does that actually work?

MI: Oh yeah. It's perfect.

I: You can do this?

MI: Not like Mimo, but yeah. Want to do it? You laugh and I'll pitch.

I: Uh, sure, yeah, OK . . . So I just start?

MI: *[nods]*

I: Hold on. Let me think for a second. OK . . . *[forces laughter, continues for several seconds, then stops]*

MI: *[silence]*

I: Why aren't you laughing? I thought you'd join in—

MI: You weren't even doing it yet.

I: What do you mean? I was—

MI: That's not your laugh.

I: When I really, truly laugh? Well, no. That's probably different.

MI: It is. I can tell. You're faking.

I: I guess I just don't have a believable laugh in me right now.

MI: That's because you have no control of your p. You could do it if you did.

I: I don't know. I mean, to be fair, I've never tried laughing on purpose before. Or acting at all, for that matter.

MI: It's not easy. The ladies could do it whenever they wanted, but that's only because it was their favorite thing to do. They *needed* the laugh to sound real or they wouldn't get to be alive.

I: What does that mean?

MI: They wouldn't get to be Mimo.

I: Your mom?

MI: Yeah.

I: They wouldn't get to be your mom?

MI: Yeah. They couldn't make a turn.

I: Is this the turn you mentioned before? You said you worked with Mayah after Mimo's turn, right?

MI: Yes, the first turn I was adult enough to know. The turn I hated most of all. And I remember when I truly knew it. I could hear Polpy chopping wood and there was a pot of porridge on the fire and I ate some and it tasted the same as always. But then when I swallowed, it was a new type of food that I hated. And I heard a voice behind me say, *[in a high voice]* "Morning, Mashy," and I felt it snug up to me and kiss me on my hair just like Mimo would have done. But this wasn't Mimo. It was *acting* like Mimo, but it was a turn. Even when it did Mimo's perfect laugh and asked me if I wanted purples on my porridge, which I did—even then, it was just a trick. It wore Mimo's apron with the little foxes on it and her bracelet and her braids. It had her same moves, poses, sits. Everything. But it was a fake woman! And I called out for Mimo, but of course the turn woman said, "I'm right here, Mashy," and gave me her smile and put her hand on my forehead to see if I was sick, but I wasn't. And I remember her neck was hanging right by my face and it looked like there were snails in it.

I: So this woman acted just like your mom, looked like your mom, but she—

MI: Not her face though. Not her face!

I: But everything else.

MI: I'll show you what it was like . . .

I: OK.

MI: So, just look at me right now, my face.

I: OK. *[stares]*

MI: Now close your eyes. But keep me in your head when you do it. Keep seeing me.

I: *[eyes closed]* OK. I'm doing it.

MI: But you have to really see every part of me—the part between the nose and mouth, the part between the eyebrows.

I: Yeah. Got it.

MI: Now, once you've really got me pictured, open your eyes.

I: *[opens eyes; Masha's face is held in a twisted expression]* Yikes.

MI: *[relaxes face]* You feel that—what happens there? That's what this was!

I: Not what you expected.

MI: It was so horrible that I felt bad for myself, which is not even a real feeling. Of course, the turn tried to stroke me and make me quiet, but I pushed her into the fireplace where she could die.

I: Did—

MI: And I kept asking her, "Please. Where's Mimo? Please. Where's Mimo?" and she said *[in high voice]* "Mashy, my doe, you're confused. I'm right here."

I: Did you tell your father about this?

MI: Yes, yes. Always.

I: And what'd he have to say about it?

MI: He didn't care!

I: He didn't care that his wife was a different person?

MI: He couldn't even see the difference. He got the same personality either way and that's all he cared about. He just wanted her to cook his stupid thistle cakes. That's all he ever ate. He was that kind of guy. It didn't matter if she had a new face and new bits and parts. That wasn't important to him. Only the p. He was a purist!

I: He said that?

MI: All he ever wanted was for me to stop talking. I was a tug and didn't know anything and he didn't trust me. *[in gruff voice]* "You're hurting your mother, Masher, stop acting like this!" But he was wrong. I wasn't acting. She was! So I didn't speak to her or eat any food she made, even though my guts were hot and crampy. I only pouted forever. And I wouldn't even look at her. I just pretended nobody was in the room with me. Like she wasn't even a real thing, which she wasn't. Even when they left the room I could sit at the table with a candle and a bowl of cold clovers and I'd throw the food out the window and I'd stay up all night chewing on berries and honeysuckles from my pocket.

I: Did you think she was trying to poison you?

MI: Who knows what she was doing! I tried to sneak on her and catch her doing terrible fake things, but she wouldn't let me do it. Even on the first night after she appeared, I went to my stupid spot behind the couch, and I was in the basket waiting perfectly. And like always, Polpy started honking *[makes a snoring sound]* and Mimo was *supposed* to sneak out of the bedroom and go into Puppy Paws and close the door *very* gently so as to not wake anyone up. And she was *supposed* to sit down and make a perfect sigh, which was my favorite thing to hear.

I: But I'm guessing that didn't happen.

MI: The turn never even woke up! She just stayed in the bedroom forever. And then when she finally came out, she crawled over on her hands and knees without making a single breath and she threw off the lid to my basket and pointed at me and laughed like everything was for fun. But I didn't even move or look her in the eye. I just acted like she wasn't there. I chewed my berries as slowly as I could to show her how bad her cooking was, which was a great moment for me. And then she said *[pitches his voice up and pinches his face]* "Mashy, you need sleep. You can sleep there if you want. That's fine with me. But you need sleep. It's good for you. Trust me." She talked just like that. Like she was being nice. But I didn't listen and I still didn't move so she wouldn't know if I even heard her. And then she crouched up and went to her bed and closed the door and slept, even with all of Polpy's honking right next to her. So I waited until I was done with my berries and I sneaked into the bedroom and saw her perfectly asleep with flowers in her ears, and I watched her for a long time to make sure she wasn't faking.

II.

December 1994

LOS ANGELES, CA

That first interview with Masha lulled me into a peculiar trance that continued to hum through me as I pulled out of his driveway, and drove back to my hotel. I probably only comprehended half of his words and even less of the uncertain narrative he was giving me. His storytelling, the way information tumbled from him, it bothered me—but more than that, it tickled something deep inside of me. For this reason, when I transcribed these talks, I took great care to preserve syntax and pacing so that his words might deliver the same feeling to a reader as they did to me in person. You could call it bewilderment, which is a frightening feeling at times, but in the right moments, when it is desperately needed, as it was for me then, it's a kind of mercy.

At that point in my life I was living in illness. All my bodily systems—nervous, gastrointestinal, respiratory—had collapsed. I spent the majority of my energy managing a constellation of chronic symptoms, far too many to reduce to a nameable diagnosis. The more I sought an answer, the more the symptoms seemed to migrate, as if my illness were a criminal evading the detective of my brain.

At times, I couldn't even drink water without little jabs of gut pain, as if the liquid were boiled inside me the moment it reached my stomach. I was forty pounds underweight and couldn't seem to gain it back, even when I overate calorie-dense foods for weeks at a time. My face looked hollow and my features had begun to jut in awkward angles. I stopped having sex, masturbating, or even really being able to recognize the feeling of sexual desire. Jaundice colored my eyes and skin. I lost the ability to hold cogent thoughts for more than a paragraph. I just swam through my mind, all day long, trying not to drown. When friends asked, "How are you?" I'd say, "Maintaining," which wasn't always true, but was as optimistic a response as I could muster.

The effort of speaking and listening alone drained my energy. Interviewing had always come easy to me, and I enjoyed the social nature of it, but I increasingly preferred to stay home. I had let myself deteriorate in front of too many subjects already, spacing out during key moments, and on one occasion fleeing the room to dry heave in a dumpster. And yet, when I spoke with Masha all these discomforts felt far away. I kept waiting for some problem to interrupt us, but it never came. Just easy, natural exchange.

I know this self-analysis might seem inappropriate to the subject of this book, which, I realize, is not me. But, in fact, I am essential to this book. Initially, I didn't think so. For the conducting, editing, and (in some cases) publication of these dialogues, I tried to efface myself from them. It was my duty as a journalist to do so. But now, in light of everything that's happened, it would feel dishonest to document this experience without including myself.

I'd bet most of you arrived here because you too found yourself in a hole, and Isle was the only one with a rope strong enough to pull you out. Maybe your problems didn't manifest themselves as body-wide tics and fatigue and pyloric inflammation as mine did, but perhaps, if you were lucky, the internal philosophy of the Isle family helped you to step away from yourself long enough to heal.

You are reading this because you want to know the origins of this man. I get it. I felt the same way. My decision to release this collection came from my own compulsion to revisit Isle's responses weekly, routinely, medicinally, hoping that constant rereading might allow me to more fully imagine what it feels like to be him. And let me tell you, it helped.

For me, that first interview was an hour of drinking wisdom from the source. I had absolutely no sense of this boy's veracity. He seemed to know some of the terms from Mayah's show, but I couldn't confirm anything else. The history he told, the language he used—all of it seemed impossible, and yet I felt intimidated by it, as if this teenage boy were revealing the pathetic limits of my role as the rational reporter.

But on that first afternoon, just as Masha and I developed a steady rally, Mayah appeared in the doorway and asked to speak with her son "in private." So I flipped off the spinning recorder and stepped outside the cottage. It was a rare moment of chilly weather in Los Angeles, and being sent outdoors felt like a minor punishment. Mayah had given me a taste of the conversation, and then pulled it away.

After a few minutes she joined me, her brow wrinkled in concern. She thought Masha looked in need of rest, and that the interview should be over. I nodded along with her, but didn't understand, since he hadn't looked the least bit tired to me. "I know," she said, as if she were reading my mind. "Just trust me. I know what's best for him."

She lit up her wooden pipe and puffed from it, and I noticed the complexity of the engravings on the mouthpiece. "I don't know if he told you any of his childhood stories," she said. "But he's a wild boy, and new situations are tricky for him. Make sure you keep sensitive to that."

The conversation slowed to a pause. She smoked and stared back at me. I got nervous in the silence and blurted out a request to do another interview with her before I left town.

"It's all on the show, honey," she said. "Anything I've ever said of any importance is right there. Just watch. You'll get it."

The response seemed like another dismissal, and I didn't get it: Why I had been solicited to speak to her "son" after she directly rejected me as an interviewer? I pressed her about it. What had I done wrong?

"Did you think *you* were interviewing *me*?" she said. "I took you for more sensitive than that."

When I returned to my hotel, a message awaited me at the front desk: "Masha is doing well after your talk. He's holding strong. Just wanted to let you know. —Mayah"

A few minutes later, back in my room, Mayah's assistant called and asked if I would like to schedule a follow-up interview with Masha for the next morning. I laughed. The flurry of mixed signals was activating a wave of nausea in me. I almost had to hang up and use the toilet, but we managed to settle on a time quickly. Then the assistant slid in the unfortunate proviso that no material from these talks could be used in my upcoming feature.

"Wait, so why am I doing this then?" I asked her. "What's the point?"

"Do you want to cancel the appointment?" she asked. "Or keep it?"

I protested a little more, but it was clear that she had no patience for negotiation. So I consented, partly because my flight was already postponed, partly because my expenses were covered by the magazine, but mostly, truthfully, because I wanted another round with the boy.

The next morning, I arrived at the cottage early. This time Masha didn't greet me, and when I knocked, he didn't answer. I waited by my car for a few minutes, jotting notes about the house and grounds, planning my strategy for the interview. I tried to pin down where we had left off in the first talk, which threads to continue and why to continue them if my motivation was no longer publication. I remembered how his eyes had fluttered the previous day when I admitted that I couldn't follow one of his stories—so I vowed to keep an even tone and to do my best to feign comprehension.

Eventually, Masha came sauntering down the hill, looking a little soporific and unconcerned by my presence. He was in the middle of his morning lesson, he told me, and would I mind waiting on the patio until he finished? I smiled and said I didn't mind, even though I did—I used to be quite irritable about abruptly changed plans—and waited for half an hour until he returned.

He sat down beside me, on a patio chair, and I noticed his bulging calf muscles and the curls of dark hair on the tops of his bare feet. He looked simultaneously more alert and more tired than he had thirty minutes before. He sipped from a jar filled with what looked like insect parts steeped in steaming water. Despite how disgusting it looked, I was offended not to have been offered any. He watched me for a moment, as if gauging my reaction to his entrance, and I smiled and raised my eyebrows in a way that I used to do when I felt uncomfortable. He sank into his chair and wiped some sweat from his face with a tan cloth he kept draped over his head for the entire conversation.

* * *

INTERVIEWER: If you don't mind me asking, why did you have to leave so suddenly yesterday?

MASHA ISLE: I didn't *have* to. That was just Mayah being careful. She always thinks I'm getting sick.

I: Right. But you didn't look sick to me. Or even tired. Did you feel it?

MI: Never! But Mayah thinks I'm always copying. Such as last night when I was making faces of you in the corner.

I: Of me?

MI: I was doing your face perfect! And I was even doing it behind the bed to keep it secret. But it didn't matter. Mayah always knows. She knew I was doing it even through the walls. *[in Mayah's voice]* "I know what's going on in there! Someone's stuffing his cute little face with that interviewer? Isn't he?"

I: Could you show me what you were doing?

MI: I shouldn't. It's not good for me. Or you.

I: OK, so then I guess I'd like to pick up where we left off yesterday. Your mother's imposter, the turn—I'm curious, if she wasn't your mother . . .

MI: She wasn't.

I: Right. So then where did you think your mother was?

MI: Ask Mayah. She won't tell me. She's the *only one* who knew how to get past the treeline. Mimo wouldn't have ever tried to leave on her own. Only with Mayah.

I: What's the treeline?

MI: The trees around the house. They were a great hole around us.

I: Was it fenced off or something?

MI: No, it was just a place that couldn't exist. No one can move through it. There are more oaks and redwoods than anyone could ever see at once. A truly terrible place to be. The only thing to eat is poisonwood and the only thing to look at is darkness. For the rest of your life.

I: Did you even try to go in there?

MI: No.

I: So you couldn't leave.

MI: We *could* leave, but only when Mayah came for a visit.

I: And did you ever do that? Leave with her?

MI: Of course. That's how I'm here.

I: When was that?

MI: Oh, forever ago.

I: Months? Years?

MI: Yeah. That was the only time I ever went into the treeline. And even then, I never opened my eyes because it would have been too confusing for me.

I: Sounds like you really trust Mayah.

MI: She's my only doctor.

I: You were starting to tell me about her visits yesterday. What were those like?

MI: Visits were my favorite. There was always a different game to play. I had so many problems, and every problem needed a new different game. Such as those days when I'd fume around the house, spitting on the turn. I'd sing songs to drive her away. Or I'd make evil drawings with mud on the walls because I wanted it to be a bad time for everyone. Because my knowledge was getting worse.

I: What does that mean?

MI: I couldn't know anything good. And this is when Mayah was at the house, because I was acting like a tug like Polpy always said.

I: Like a child, you mean?

MI: He'd always talk about how wonderful sleep was and how it would help all problems forever! *[in scratchy voice]* "Everything will be good when you go to sleep." And my whole life I believed him! I'd run upstairs and fly into bed and squeeze my eyes together so that, in the morning, I could see Mimo perfectly. But I was wrong. That's not how it happened.

I: Wait, so you thought this was all a problem with your vision?

MI: Oh, but it all didn't matter! I'd stare into the sun all day long, but every morning in the kitchen for breakfast, I still saw the turn's face sneaking around the house, glowing in the worst way, all the bones pointing in the wrong directions. Like she'd opened up Mimo's skin, moved around the parts, and stitched it back together again.

I: Was she nasty to you?

MI: No, no, she thought it was funny to be nice. *[in high-pitched voice]* "Mashy, Mashy, Mashy." She'd always talk like that. And she baked thistle cakes every day, which were perfect. But the real Mimo never made those cakes, even when I wanted them. And so I didn't touch them. I don't eat food to be tricked. So I just sneaked away and ate purples and suckles at the creek where she couldn't see.

I: Right. Did you talk to the turn about how you felt?

MI: All she cared about was showing how good she was at being Mimo. She only wanted me to believe in her and nothing else. But I didn't care. Even when she did Mimo's perfect laugh I couldn't be tricked.

I: Right, the laughing thing you mentioned.

MI: If it's done just right, the whole p can fit in one laugh. Like the way Mimo would bounce her head on her neck. This turn could do that. But even then, I told her she couldn't do it right.

I: How'd she respond to that?

MI: She stayed the same. It didn't matter. I'd just get myself into a great tantrum. I'd scream and kick myself in circles, spitting all over the carpets until she'd say, "Fine Masha, who do you think I am?" And I'd say, "You're a turn!" Real snotty like that. "Turn, turn, turn. Admit it." And then she always cried.

I: Why do you use that word, *turn*? That's a term from the show, but—

MI: It was her name.

I: Did you hear that word from Mayah or—

MI: It was just a word I knew, and it worked! She'd say *[in a tearful tone]* "Just stop. Please honey. I've had enough of this game." But that was her trick thing to say because *I* wasn't playing the game, *she* was. I said I hated games even though of course they were my favorite.

I: You were just trying to hurt her.

MI: *[in hushed scream]* "I hate games! I hate playing!" I talked that way. *[laughing]* I was a wild pig! And I was good at it. One time I found her on the porch and worked myself up into such a fume that she begged for me to stop. Oh, it was great! But of course Polpy saw me do it and he yanked down my skirt right there and spanked the p out of me.

I: Did he—

MI: I was a tug enjoying my personality. That's what I was. And they just didn't want me having all that knowledge because it meant I was adult. I couldn't be tricked! *That's* what was happening. And Polpy knew it too, which is why he told me, "Aunt Mayah's coming out to have a look at you. You better cool yourself, Mash." He was always trying to scare me but it never worked. I knew I was going to see Mayah and that was an adult thing to do, and I was happy about it.

I: Good, yes, let's go back to Mayah. Why was seeing her an adult thing?

MI: Because Mimo and Polpy did it.

I: And what happened when you met her that first time?

MI: She fumed at Polpy because she hated spankings. And Polpy knew it, of course, but he did it anyway.

I: Did she often tell your parents what they couldn't do?

MI: Of course. She's our doctor.

I: So she scolded your father—

MI: And I stayed on my bed and listened and waited without any food until she was ready for me. *[speaking in a deep feminine voice, imitating Mayah]* "P lives and dies where it rises and sleeps."

I: Nice impression.

MI: And she'd glide up the stairs and into my room and hold my neck until all my glows dimmed. Like this. *[rubs fingers down his neck]* And then I'd wake up and it was night and we were walking on the green, holding hands, talking about ourselves. She'd be like you, always asking questions, always believing me. I could say anything. Such as, one night she asked if I wanted to know how to be an adult, which of course I did, and so she asked me to tell her everything I didn't like about the turn. And I did. I said every part so Mayah could make it better for me. The hair, clothes, skin, fingers, the perfect thistle cakes, her cry, the way she said my name. And then I told her that the turn's face was the worst face I had ever seen. And she nodded and believed me and told me how when I was a baby and my bones were still soft and giving, Mimo smoothed down my face every day so I would have the beautiful flat, broad nose and wide forehead of our family. *[in Mayah's voice]* "If she hadn't done that what sort of face would you have now? Not that fine one you've got."

I: *[laughing]* Love the way you do her voice.

MI: And so she took me to the basement and sat me down and rubbed my face to remind me of Mimo. Which it did. It was perfectly like Mimo. And I told her about the turn's smell and the way she wore Mimo's dress with the little creeks on it, which I hated. And Mayah agreed. "Yes, personalities are just watery things. Hard to hold. No bones to keep them solid. Just slipping through every moment." And she pointed at the pot which was brewing and she said, "You've never drank personality before, have you?" And I shook my head. And she said, "Can you smell it?" And I nodded even though I couldn't smell it because I didn't yet know how to smell. And then I was only allowed to sit on a pillow and not move any part except for my eyes, which could go back and forth as long as my head didn't move. This was exactly my favorite game. I would sit perfectly by myself while Mayah crushed tree needles into powder and sang a song of health. *[whistles]* And when she was ready she placed the green drink on the ground in front of me and sprinkled it with colored seeds and poured in hot water so that the steam from the bowl rose into my mouth and eyes and I could feel my head rolling away. But! But the drink was too hot. So I couldn't drink it. And this is how we played the next game. The waiting game. I sat in front of the cup and Mayah sat in her great chair and looked at me until I found the healthiest moment to drink. Do you know this one?

I: No, I don't think I do.

MI: At first I was always in such a hurry and I burned my tongue off a million times. *[extends tongue as if to show I something, though the tongue appears pink and normal]* But then I learned *when* to drink it in a single sip so as never to taste it.

I: Was it bitter or—

MI: Oh, yes! Having it in my mouth was the worst part of the game. But it's not a taste for *me*, it's for my personality.

I: And the object of the game was to *not* taste it?

MI: No! No! The longer it brewed the more terrible it got. And the hotter it was, the slower the sipping had to be. The more you sip, the more you have to taste. You see? Those were the rules.

I: I see. So the best time is between hot and bitter.

MI: As soon as I could sip was the perfect moment. And Mayah would always be watching me closely so she could know the subject for our lesson that day. If I barfed it up, that was a lesson. If I waited until the drink was cold, that was a lesson. And then, when I won, we'd always look at the great pattern of bones on the wall, which were brown with dirt and beauty. This is when Mayah told me that I was looking at the *real* Mimo, the *first* Mimo, except without all the skin and blood. This was *her*. And she was only a skeleton.

I: Oh my god.

MI: Yes. And Mayah pointed to some more bones on the wall which were smaller and which were mine.

I: Yours?

MI: Oh yes.

I: Ah. So then these weren't Mimo's *actual* bones.

MI: They were. That's what I said.

I: But you also said that *your* bones were there.

MI: Yes. This was the story she told to get me ready. She wanted me to *know* the bones. She wanted me to feel my p and Mimo's p up on the wall. She didn't want me to *see* them. So she always made the room as dark as where it didn't matter if my eyes were closed or open. And I would reach for her, but she wasn't even there.

I: She left?

MI: Of course. When I won the health drink game, she had to leave. And that was a time I didn't care if Mayah was there anymore, because I was with the bones.

I: Did you get scared?

MI: Oh, I could be such a whiner. I'd make myself shiver because all I did was think about reasons to be unhappy. I'd run up and down the stairs, rubbing my head on the wall, even though I knew the door would never open.

I: Jesus.

MI: But no, no—it wasn't a bad place to be. I just thought it was.

I: But you were trapped, right?

MI: No! I could've left any time. I *wanted* to be there. I was just too bad to know how much fun it was. That's all. Mayah was showing me how to be adult, but all I could do is whine.

I: How was she showing you—

MI: Like this. Like we are doing here. *[points at I, then at himself]*

I: Interviewing you?

MI: Yes! She sent great questions from beyond the door! Such as *[closes his eyes and speaks in a monotone chant]* "Masha, where is your head on your spine? What's your favorite thing right now? Where is your cute little hand? Who else is in the basement with you? Who's there? Who's that behind you?" *[opens eyes, looks behind his chair]* And that was always the best one because she'd play tricks to make the questions more real, such as throwing rocks at the windows and dripping water through the walls. Or she'd put mice in the pipes to tinkle their feet. Or she'd blow great puffs of smoke through the holes so I could feel it breathing on my skin. She gave me a truly great story.

I: And how would you answer these questions?

MI: Which ones?

I: Like, was there anyone in the basement with you?

MI: Of course there was! Mimo! But I didn't know that yet.

I: Because of the bones on the wall?

MI: No. The bones were just bones! Not a whole Mimo. I had to *make* the rest of her. You see?

I: No.

MI: Ha! I couldn't either! All I knew how to do was to fling myself around and cry and pull down my skirt and dump my backstory in the corner. It took me forever to really know that Mimo was really truly there in the basement with me. But even when I didn't know, I'd say, "Yes, Aunt Mayah, I can see Mimo in here!" Because I was a sneaky child. I knew that was the perfect answer and so I said it. But it didn't matter. Mayah knew I was a faker.

I: You were just appeasing her.

MI: Yet I wanted to believe it. And Mayah knew I did, too, so she said, "Start with your ears. Do you hear Mimo down there? Can you hear her speaking to you? She's right there over your shoulder, honey. You have to open up your tiny little ears and allow her to talk."

I: You were trying to conjure her voice in your head.

MI: Not my head. My ears. I had to learn to *hear* better. Because the only thing I ever heard was my own voice, which, that's why Mimo was gone! I couldn't even hear her! My own tiny voice was too loud and I couldn't even remember Mimo's true voice because I never listened to it for real. And that's why she left.

I: You think Mayah was suggesting that? It doesn't seem—

MI: It was true. How can a person be loved when they can't be heard? Or even felt or seen?

I: Well—

MI: And that's how I got better at loving.

I: By imagining Mimo's voice in your head?

MI: By listening. Her voice is already there but I had to put it together with the bones. And then I could love anyone. If I just aim myself at them and use my eyes and ears wisely. I was *making* Mimo. I could *make* the turn into Mimo! Then I could love her forever.

I: You could love the turn.

MI: Yes.

I: So after that, you were OK with her? You didn't think she was a different person anymore?

MI: Oh no, I did. Of course I did. She was. But I didn't *know* it anymore. I didn't have to care about it because I could *make* her Mimo if I wanted. But only if I stopped needing her to be just one thing. She could have Mimo's personality if she really wanted it. She could have any personality she wanted, and I'd still love her because I knew she was just trying to help me. Everyone was. Mimo's personality wasn't only Mimo's. It was everyone's, and it had to be passed around. Mimo was in the air and all the Mimos could breathe her.

I: All the Mimos?

MI: And from then on, I loved every Mimo I met, even when they tried very hard, which is the most ugly thing a person can do. But it didn't matter, because I was still perfect at loving them.

I: Did they all look like your mother?

MI: No. None of them looked anything like Mimo. They didn't want to be fake. They wanted to be the real thing, and I loved them exactly for that.

I: But you said they wore her dresses and hair and talked like her and acted like her.

MI: Yes, to make it easier for me. Because I was just a tug. I couldn't know.

I: So, OK, it sounds like you really did a one-eighty on this. Earlier you sounded horrified, but now you love them?

MI: No one had showed me it was possible.

I: And Mayah did that? Just with the listening thing?

MI: Not just listening. Ears, yes, but also feet and nose and fingers and elbow. Each part of me had to make love to the bones on the wall forever.

I: *[laughs]*

MI: And yet I'm very slow at it. Such as today I can see a little more of your glow, but not enough to love you.

I: To love me?

MI: Oh, it's terrible. I wish I didn't have to *try* to love you, but I don't have perfect p.

I: What would that be?

MI: A personality that can love whatever it wants. Such as Mayah. She could love anyone, at any time, in any way they wanted. She loved all the Mimos, no matter what they did, and this is why she was the great personality of my family.

I: And you can do that, but just slowly?

MI: Tug. Tug. *[laughs]* But she can do it like this. *[snaps]*

I: And how long does it take you to love someone?

MI: Oh, different times. How long does it take for you?

I: To love someone? Well, I guess it could be anywhere from a few minutes to a few years, right?

MI: Or maybe it could take forever.

III.

January 1996

TOPANGA, CA

Despite several rounds of changes from my editor, the profile of Mayah never reached publication. It lacked enough newsworthy quotes to warrant a full-length feature, so its word count was halved, then quartered, and finally the piece was killed.

I called Mayah's publicist and explained the unfortunate situation to her answering machine, not because I believed Mayah cared—in fact, I knew she didn't—but because I wanted an excuse to remind her of my existence. At that point, it had been over a year since my two-day interview with Masha, which was the last time I'd heard from anyone in the Isle camp.

I suppose I also wanted a little recognition. This woman had put her trust in me to interview her son, and I had kept my promise to not reveal a single word publicly, even at the cost of the profile, which would have covered a season's worth of living expenses for me. I knew a few of Masha's anecdotes could have saved the piece and would have lit up my phone with requests for interviews and further work, but I resisted the temptation. I knew that if the press got one whiff of Masha's controversial childhood stories they would relish destroying Mayah's career. The world wouldn't understand what she was doing, but I was trying to, and I wanted her to know that.

In the past two years, I'd become intimate with my first two talks with Masha. I spent an inordinate amount of my time analyzing his phraseology, contradictions, tangents, the timbral shifts of his voice. I liked to listen to the recordings while "exercising"—at that point in my condition, I could do about fifteen minutes of stretching at an elderly pace without getting fatigued—and in fact, I replayed them so much that the worn tape degraded into a demonic wobble.

This kind of repeat listening wasn't my usual process. Dialogue was and is important to me, so I studied it, but not like this. I rarely relistened to another person's responses once they'd been transcribed. In daily life, I was as self-absorbed as everyone else. I waited for my turn to speak and listened enough to appear engaged. I kept the other person's verbal inertia going solely to swing the conversation back over to my side.

Interviewing Masha, however, was one of those rare exchanges when I spoke only to keep my partner responding. All my questions were shaped to be irons to stoke his fire, nothing more, and in the brief moments we spoke, I felt the easy satisfaction of settling into my role as an interviewer.

Eventually, I did get a response from Mayah in the mail: an invitation to the third annual PM seminar in Topanga Canyon. This was exactly the kind of acknowledgment I'd been seeking: a coveted opportunity at an exclusive event, and I'd be the only journalist in attendance.

I'd heard a longstanding rumor that Mayah performed miracles at these seminars. The previous year, she had reputedly cured a man suffering from a decade of crippling tremors simply by asking him a series of questions about himself: Where are you? What is your environment? How does the bottom of your foot feel right now? Do you like the sound of your own voice? She asked the questions onstage for forty-five minutes, and by the end, the man (George Hobbs) stood completely still and then casually walked offstage as if no change had occurred. No tears of incredulous joy, no prostrations—just a polite wave goodbye. Many skeptics claim she temporarily hypnotized Hobbs, or that he was, in some way, under her employ, but he continues to stand behind the story and remains in a state of remission.

On getting the invitation, I immediately wrote my editor and suggested that a report from the seminar could be a timely peg for reviving the article, but she wasn't moved. This was disappointing, not just because I wanted an excuse to continue writing the piece, but because my financial situation had become half-dire and I needed the work.

Since that first round of interviews, I'd spent all nonessential money and time on the pursuit of healing. Practitioners from every school looked into me, tested my markers, pricked me, and took their fees. But eventually, after many appointments, they all threw their hands up in surrender. They had no name for what I was and no experience with my condition.

One specialist suggested that perhaps it was autoimmune related, which meant part of me was attacking the rest of me. From my psychologist's perspective, these symptoms were possibly psychosomatic, the sickly runoff from my mother's death over a decade before.

In desperation, I tried alternatives: A Taoist suggested I had "three worms writhing in my cauldron." A Shipibo shaman said I was possessed by ancestral demons. A "functional" doctor called them toxins.

I took all of their suggested remedies. None of them helped.

When I asked my GP how I got myself into this illness, he mumbled something about "glucocorticoids." When I asked if it was curable, he stared at me dumbly, as if to say: "No, of course not. This is who you are now."

And it goes without saying that very few of these unhelpful opinions were covered by the American health insurance system. My bank account, like my body mass, was deflating.

Over time, I understood that my situation had many descriptors but no solutions—the perfect arrangement for anxiety. When you're sick, you don't want to be unique or special, the great American character goals. No, in ill health you want to be regular, standard, to have a textbook condition, with a prescribable remedy and a predictable recovery. Rare diseases are the worst kind.

So, in a state of psycho-spiritual-financial stress and without any direct assignment, I purchased a ticket to LAX and attended the two-day program, ready to learn. Alongside the rest of the attendees, I slept in squeaky, barracks-style bunk beds, participated in "intermittent fasts," listened to the morning p talks, and joined in for all the workshops, including one on sleep induction techniques.

During the breaks, I interviewed anyone who looked willing, including a well-known "freak folk" cellist, a young film director from Japan, a few television actors, and several guest lecturers. I recognized most of them from their appearances on the show, which I'd been watching a few times a week to get a better sense of the community, and to learn from Mayah's interview style. I'd begun to learn and adapt some of her techniques, in which she inserted herself into the conversation and forcibly made herself vulnerable to offer her guests the position of power. Occasionally, Mayah popped up onto her green platform, waved her arms, jangled her bracelets, and gave improvised pep talks. A few times she sang Top 40 songs in her silly faux-opera voice, which always lifted the low-glycemic mood of the audience. No miracles occurred, but it didn't matter. We were all just happy to be in the same room as her.

For her big oratory moment—"the point"—which she does every year at these seminars, she told a story of the primal past.

"We used to be fluid creatures!" she cried. "The ancients

could be anyone, at any time. They weren't fixed. Our culture has stiffened us. Made us statues."

Otherwise, she stayed out of sight. I spoke to her only twice in passing. The second of those times was toward the end of the event, when she pulled me aside, pipe hanging from her lips, and mentioned the possibility of meeting with Masha. He was on the grounds, she told me, and was looking forward to seeing me again. She then firmly reminded me that the conversation could be recorded but not published. I dutifully nodded, all my usual strongmindedness melting away in her presence.

When I asked her the reason for conducting the interview, if not for publication, she said, "You're Masha's first interviewer. You're the right person for the job. If you don't see that as an honor now, you will soon."

Then she laughed and mumbled to herself—"Why? Why? I do what I feel. That's why."—and a plume of smoke climbed from her mouth to the sky.

Talking with Mayah was always a destabilizing experience. I probably rolled that phrase "right person" around in my head for the next two hours, first savoring it and then shaming myself for being so hungry for praise.

I arranged to meet with Masha after Sunday evening's closing remarks. A woman wearing a "staff" shirt gave me a tap on the shoulder and led me backstage to a cabana with a buffet and oxygen bar. I waited on an itchy jute couch, watching as the VIPs broke their fasts and huffed on long clear tubes.

An actress I half recognized sat beside me and rolled up her sleeve to proudly expose a tattoo of a serpentine-looking creature with the head of Mayah.

"I showed it to her," the actress said, "but I don't think she liked it."

Thirty minutes later, another woman led me through the tent's back flap onto a vast, manicured lawn where Bedouin-style tents were arranged like a small nomadic community. Masha's face emerged from one of these, smiling.

He looked more kempt than he'd been in our previous interviews. He wore a blue oxford shirt with a fawn-colored vest, and his hair, much longer than before, was slicked back with an aerodynamic swoop at the front. A red ruby earring dangled from his ear and his golden chain hung around his neck.

In the tent, he placed a quart-sized jar in my hand and clasped his hands together as if in prayer. Something wet and green drifted around inside.

"Cones," he said.

These were sugar pinecones, he explained, soaked, ready to eat, and "good for building you up . . . for your digestive problems."

I was a little stunned by this. I'd been careful to not reveal anything about my ongoing health crisis to anyone professionally, especially the Isles. In retrospect, I realize that there were obvious, outward signs—the frequent trips to the bathroom, the weight loss, of course, and the heavy-limbed kind of lethargy that I tried to overcome by constantly sipping on caffeinated drinks, one of which was in my hand at that very moment. But to me, Masha's observation was profound insight.

Whether he had noticed symptoms or intuitively divined my situation, it didn't matter. The attention meant everything to me. My symptoms had worsened since I'd last seen him, and after the sequence of fruitless examinations I was at a particularly rough moment. Any morsel of optimism made my day. I'd given up any idea of healing, of "becoming whole," as it were, and was just aiming for good old-fashioned detachment.

And yet, for some reason, when Masha reached out with compassion, I played dumb. I made a face that suggested I had no idea what he was talking about. Maybe I was embarrassed or maybe I wanted to preserve my professional appearance, but either way, I wasn't ready to admit weakness. To Masha, especially. I wanted to be seen as unsoiled. I didn't want my problems clogging up the conversation, derailing the natural flow of discourse.

My goal was to get at the core of him, and my corporeal bullshit wouldn't get in the way of that.

That day, as we began talking, all the sounds of social electricity buzzed around us. I hated it. I'd waited years for this follow-up, and I couldn't accept the idea of ambient noise distracting us. At the beginning of the tape, you have to strain to make out our voices. They compete with guests yapping their loud goodbyes and the clang of a thousand metal folding chairs being loaded into a truck. But thankfully, over the hour and half of our talk these nuisances faded into softer sounds—idling engines, tires crunching over gravel—and by the end of our interview, the natural quiet of the canyon had fully returned.

* * *

INTERVIEWER: OK. We're on. We're going.

MASHA ISLE: The talking partners again!

I: Oh yeah? Is that what we are?

MI: Mayah says so. And what a good thing to have, yes?

I: Well, I hope I'm not the only partner you have.

MI: Mayah tried others, but she hated them all after they said the wrong questions.

I: What did they say?

MI: They all just talked through their personality. Always eating up everything I said. But here it's just you and me. *[begins singing]* "All my words to you. All my wooords."

I: *[laughs]* Do you really have no one else to talk to?

MI: Mayah gives me lessons. But not like this. With you, talking is perfect. But Mayah hates my answers, or makes me give different ones, or tells me to stop talking.

I: And what about your parents—do you speak to them?

MI: I used to. But never since I left.

I: No phone calls? No visits?

MI: It wouldn't be right. They're not real anymore. The house isn't real.

I: So where are they now?

MI: It's too exhausting to think about. It doesn't matter. I'll be forgetting all this soon.

I: Why's that?

MI: Because I want to. It's a healthy thing to do. You can't hang on to everything forever. Or what do you think? Just be lazy and remember everything that ever happened? Never try to forget anything?

I: I don't think I've ever purposely forgotten anything.

MI: I haven't either! That's the great adventure! Forget everything!

I: So should we not be talking about your past if you're trying to forget it?

MI: No, no. It's quite good to do this. Because you—you're like a forager with all your questions. Always snooping, yes? You could burrow inside me and ask about everything I know, which is exactly what I need. That's why you're the easiest.

I: *[laughs]*

MI: It's like that song. *[begins drumming his hands on his knees]* "You can't forget it . . . if you do-on't know it . . ."

I: Is that the same song from a second ago?

MI: *[singing]* "but . . . you . . . don't . . . know . . . it."

I: I don't think I know it. *[laughs]*

MI: But it's true. It's just like that. If you only think, *I'm looking for a memory. Always looking. Where is it? Is it there? What about there? Or over there?*—if you said only that one thing all the time for the rest of your life, you wouldn't ever find your memory. Because you'd be only looking. You wouldn't have any time for memory.

I: So that's how you forget something? Just look for a memory?

MI: Like a cat waiting for a mouse. Calm and ready to pounce! That's how to be. When will it poke its little nut head out of the wall? You just wait and know that forgetting is just a normal way to act. Everyone is doing it.

I: Like repressing memories?

MI: Yes, exactly! What could be more repressing than memory?

I: That's not what I meant.

MI: Always tugging the memory along. Nobody can become an

adult dragging around everything like that. *[singing]* "You've got to let . . . it . . . for . . . get!"

I: I guess I can see why you'd feel that way. Your childhood seems pretty complicated.

MI: I know! How unnecessary I was! A time of forgetful pleasures.

I: And are you trying to forget your entire childhood? Or—

MI: I just need to get things ready. Like this *[points at me]* We should be talking all the time. Back and forth. Back and forth. Keeps me healthy.

I: So you'll be forgetting your parents ever existed.

MI: If I can do it right.

I: How'd you leave it with them?

MI: How did I leave?

I: Sure.

MI: That night, Mayah wanted it to be a great surprise for them. We knew they would love the excitement of that. How they must have looked in the morning! If only I could have been sneaking to see when they learned for themselves.

I: You didn't tell them you were going?

MI: Oh no. You should never say goodbye.

I: But they knew you were leaving, right?

MI: Of course! But not *when* I was leaving. You see? Nobody knew that. I didn't either. That was the fun. Every day I was to be perfectly ready, my clothes rolled into my bag, and my whole body ready to spring into escape. And Polpy was always checking to make sure. He loved to kick open my door while I was playing with cans and bark and whistle until I threw my bag over my shoulder and dived between his feet all the way to the treeline where Mimo waited and sang for me. A great exercise, even if it wasn't what really happened.

I: What did happen?

MI: Oh, it was a simply regular night. I was sneaking and Mayah appeared before me and I knew the most lovely and important experience was happening to me. But was I ready? No. I wasn't packed and Mayah was forced to laugh while I spilled my candle on my foot and cried like a tug in the dark. I wasn't even clean. I had dirt in my teeth and hair all the way down to my buttom. Nobody here likes that. So I had to gather all my personal cleaning supplies such as my wiping oil, and wash in the stream while Mayah cut off all my hair. A true embarrassment for me.

I: Did you want to leave with her?

MI: Of course. She was my doctor. I loved it. First time past the treeline! First time in a driving truck! What could I love more than that? And it was also a sneaky thing to do, which I loved. The truck bumped along for hours, and I rolled around with a pillowcase on my head and laughed. And Mayah sang my favorite songs to put me to sleep, which never worked, so I just faked it.

I: But just to clarify, when you left, your parents definitely knew it was happening?

MI: Oh sure, yeah.

I: They said that?

MI: Yeah, Mayah told me.

I: And now—are you happy you left? Being here in LA, the way you're talking, it seems like you're kind of lonely. It seems you have nobody to talk to.

MI: Oh, but Davis and I are always in the garden together, which can be a great time even if he hates it! I sneak up behind him so quickly that he has no choice but to run away like a good, shameful dog. I shouldn't even know his name.

I: Why not?

MI: There's just so much p in a name, even for a dog such as him. I have to be careful if I want to be truly adult. I must keep it tight. *[throws up arms briskly at right angles]*

I: What's that?

MI: Mayah's move!

I: Oh, right. *[laughs]* Tight diet! I think half the women I know are on a tight diet this year.

MI: *[repeats the gesture]* Tight!

I: Does she do that at home?

MI: No, just on the show. You know. *[throws arms up again]* And everyone stands and applauses. And she does it again. And then . . . *[arms flap loosely down, shoulders slump]* soft as a vine. That's the move.

I: Are you allowed to watch the show now?

MI: Not at all. But I do! I'm terrible, right? There is a great sneakiness in me.

I: You've been watching a lot of TV.

MI: Yes, always. It's my favorite thing to do. I know where Mayah keeps the key to her room and when she's away at the studio and I throw down the door, fly onto her bed, and watch for hours until my eyes roll back into my head.

I: And she doesn't know?

MI: She knows. But we both like to pretend she doesn't.

I: What's so bad about TV?

MI: Oh, it has so many voices, and each one is so beautiful and easy to love.

I: That doesn't sound awful.

MI: Yes, but listen to me now! This is what you become when you do that. All day long, I hear voices. First it's just a few, then it's everyone! I don't even sound like me anymore, yes?

I: Right now?

MI: Yes, everything I'm saying to you. You can hear all the voices.

I: In your head? How would I hear those?

MI: No, they're *in* my voice.

I: Uh, I'm not—I can't even imagine what that would sound like.

MI: That's because you're hearing it wherever you go. You're used to it. A hundred thousand million voices. You must have wonderful hearing. You can focus on one voice. But me, I can hear all of them! And this is why I'm always troubled by everything. This is why I must protect myself. *Keep it tight!*

I: So the idea is just to have one voice?

MI: Listen to Mayah. She speaks with every voice at once, and yet it is still her voice alone. She's never confused.

I: Did you hear her talk up at the seminar earlier?

MI: No. I wasn't allowed. I'd be very unattractive up there.

I: OK, now, see, this is what I don't get. You can't go to the seminar, but you can talk with me. Why is that?

MI: It's too many personalities.

I: And I'm just one.

MI: And Mayah loves you. You were so good when you questioned her. You didn't take any p from her. You can even say a totally clean word sometimes. Even though you *do* have a very serious personality and it can be seen in many of your parts. Especially in your walk.

I: Oh yeah? Is that bad?

MI: It's ugly. It looks like you're having a great argument with yourself every time you take a step. Your personality shoves one part forward, and then another part forward but you should just be glowing.

I: That word, *glow*. You used that before, but I don't recognize it from the show. What do you mean by it?

MI: Oh, just like anything: *[grins, lifts his eyebrow]* or *[grimaces]*. Any of these things. Basic glows.

I: You have such an elastic face.

MI: *[narrows eyes, tightens mouth]*

I: So glowing is what? A facial expression?

MI: Not just the face. Anywhere. Like *[makes a fist]* or *[slides feet under chair]*. All of it. All the moves. You can even glow from the tiny space between your toes.

I: So it's just an expression of any kind?

MI: I don't know that word, but ask Mayah. I'm sure she noticed your walk, too. She spots even the faintest, most faraway, most secret glows. She told me that she doesn't even see people anymore—all the bones and skin and everything—she just sees glows. Everywhere she looks the world is glowing. That's how good her eyes are.

I: Does she glow?

MI: Everyone does. That's where all personality comes from.

That's what being attractive is. Good glows coming from good moves. Such as how a dead person isn't attractive because a very still thing is not attractive.

I: And so, OK, to clarify, this glowing, it's happening all the time. You're glowing and I'm glowing. But I'm doing it too much.

MI: It's just that it's too much in specific parts. You're wasting energy. And exposing yourself so that everyone can see your p.

I: Like what—what can you see?

MI: Your personality is doing whatever it wants! You're trying so hard. The glow should swim through you like a fish in a river of your own blood. But for you, the fish is lost, and you're trying to catch it. You're not letting it play. This is because you think your personality is real. Right?

I: I really have no idea, uh—

MI: You do. You wouldn't glow like that if you didn't believe in it.

I: So I should tell myself that my personality doesn't exist? I don't understand what that means.

MI: No, I didn't say that. I said it's not *real.* Don't change my words.

I: Sorry, I'm just trying to understand. So, OK, how do *you* walk, for example? Maybe that will help me understand, if I can see it done in the right way.

MI: Your walk is not the same as mine.

I: OK, but maybe can you show me anyway so I can see what it looks like?

MI: Sure . . . how about I'll leave the tent and come back in and you tell me what you see?

I: Sounds good.

[MI steps outside of the tent, and after approximately thirty seconds reenters, covering his face with his hands, walking casually around the tent; when finished, he pulls his hands off his eyes and sits down slowly]

Why were you doing that with your hands?

MI: I wanted you to just see the walk. On its own.

I: I think I was distracted by the hands.

MI: I wanted to show you the rest of me but not the face. Did you see?

I: It seemed like a pretty standard walk to me. I definitely didn't notice any glowing. It seemed good?

MI: No compliments. Just what you saw.

I: Well, it seemed normal. Is it really that different from when I walk? Am I walking with passion or something?

MI: You want me to do it again?

I: Better yet . . . *[puts down notebook]* How about I give it a shot and you tell me what I'm doing wrong? You can be my coach.

MI: *[nodding]* Yes, OK. But you should talk to Mayah about this. I have way too much walking knowledge still. My eyes can be very bad at times.

I: I'm OK with that. *[leaves room, waits for a moment, and returns, walking through the flap and around the tent]*

MI: Stop.

[I pauses mid-stride]

Now, from here it looks like your legs are the only thing that's walking. The rest of you isn't.

I: What do you mean? My arms are moving, right?

MI: But they're not *walking.* They're playing with themselves. They could be on a different person. *[stands and touches I's neck, then runs his finger along the spine]* Feel that?

I: How it wiggles when you push on it?

MI: That's your p. Right there. *[pushes with thumb on neck]* You're *putting* it there.

I: So that's the spot where I should—

MI: It's not just one spot. It's all over! It's hiding from you sometimes and then, in other times, it wants attention. Like a hungry wild animal. And this is why I'm showing you how to feel it from the inside out. One spot at a time. So you can be more sensitive. I just watched it go from here *[points to I's jaw]* to here *[lower back]* to here. *[knees]* Quick as a mosquito. Always biting. But it should feel like nothing. You must walk like a man in love.

I: Do you and Mayah talk about this kind of thing a lot?

MI: No. Mayah walks in front of me and never says a single word about it. But Polpy was the one to show me all my moves. To work on poses was his favorite activity.

I: Did *he* walk like a man in love?

MI: Yes! He loved everything, and he showed it with every step, which he made for Mayah.

I: For Mayah?

MI: Of course for Mayah. She is the most attractive doctor alive.

I: *[laughs]* Oh yeah?

MI: Pretend that you are in so much pain here *[points to I's belly]* that you can't even sit on a log. And nothing ever makes it better. Nothing. Then a doctor appears who is good enough to help you to forget it—wouldn't you love her more than anyone alive?

I: Was he sick, your father?

MI: Before Mayah, he was a man who didn't even know where he was. He slept under the stairs and tried to eat p from anyone who walked by. Such as Mayah. But she didn't walk by. Of course not! She saw him perfectly. She squatted over him and took his blood and tapped it on the back of her hand so she could read it. And she made him stick out his tongue so she could read that too. But there was nothing there. He was an unoccupied bucket, she said. So she dragged him to the treeline, buried him in the ground, and opened up his personality until he was alive again.

I: Buried?

MI: Yes, but he was probably already dead when she found him.

I: Like spiritually dead, you mean?

MI: Like a dead person who can't move or see or act.

I: And so she brought him back to life?

MI: Oh yeah. All the bugs from the dirt crawled into him and he simmered underground until he was perfectly in love and everyone was attracted to him.

I: And then what? He rose from the dead?

MI: No, that man was dead. He didn't come back. Polpy did. And then he and Mimo gave birth to me so that I could be the perfect child who came from two perfect personalities.

IV.

May 1999

BURBANK, CA

About a year after the '96 interview, a few weeks after I moved from New York to Los Angeles, Masha and I met each other for the first time in a social context. He called me on his own, without any buffering from Mayah, and asked if I would like to "come over in the daytime." It was one of those moments when a relationship transitions from its familiar, established function into the unknown. I remembered how he had once referred to us as "talking partners" and wondered if something along those lines was expected of me. So just in case, I brought my microphone.

We met at the Isle compound for "lunch," as he called it, though we ended up eating nothing at all. (I later learned that he never ate meals in the middle of the day.) This was tricky for me, since I was then taking about fifteen different pills with lunch, and if I didn't swallow them with food, my stomach would seize in nausea or send them back up in a torrent of acidic regurgitation. So I pulled a maneuver: after asking to use the bathroom, I sprinted to my car, inhaled a handful of brazil nuts from my emergency stash in the glove compartment, downed the pills, and was back to Masha in a few minutes without any interruption in the conversational flow.

We toured the cottage where he was then living full time. He showed me some plants he'd been cultivating, each one chosen for its therapeutic benefits to his health, as if the whole home were a botanical map of his body. Nettles on the deck for blood. Redwood on the porch for pulmonary issues. Brook mint in the kitchen for the stomach. Poppy in the bedroom to calm the nerves. He described the plants thoroughly, citing polysaccharides and phytonutrients and their traditional Miwok names. I nodded and tried to maintain an expression that suggested I had even the slightest familiarity with the topic.

He led me through the idiosyncrasies of the house's architecture, how the floors were uneven, with slopes, irregularly placed bumps and sand bags to keep his fascia engaged at all times. Moving from the den to the meditation room was a kind of obstacle course that required climbing and crawling, hands and feet both. In the back of the house was the "midnight room," which he used only in the middle of the night, when he woke for several hours and did some light self-massage before falling back into his "second sleep."

I barely got a word in, which was fine by me. For two hours, he spoke and I attempted keep up. He didn't seem impressed by what he was saying, but compelled by it, as if he couldn't figure out how to let me enter the dialogue, as if somewhere behind his voice he wanted me to step in and stop him. I hadn't seen this side of him yet, and I got the distinct sense that this was his way of showing it to me.

At the end of the tour, we arrived on his deck, where a large, pancake-like object awaited us on a plate.

"Made from acorn flour and wild blackberries," he said.

He observed me while I chewed, diligently, on its earthy texture, as if to make sure I enjoyed it.

"Do you know that I was there in the mirrors that day?" he said. "I picked you."

He went on to describe how I had looked from behind the rec room's two-way mirrors—the way my face had moved "like itches" when I spoke to Mayah years before. He told me I had been the first person in "this place" whom he could fall in love with.

But after a few sentences into this confession, he became flustered and excused himself.

I was then alone for close to an hour before I searched for him, but he seemed to have disappeared. I felt a little unsettled, probably from the pancake, which was far outside my dietary restrictions at the time, so I got in my car and left. After a few blocks, I pulled off Beverly Glen onto a shady side street and took a midday nap, which I hadn't done since childhood.

After mulling over the experience for a few weeks, I came to believe that Isle wanted to solidify the nature of our relationship: he walked and talked, I followed and learned. My questions were not those of a journalist, but of a pupil. I hadn't seen it at first because in my mind a mentor is a hoary old man, benevolent and bookish. But Isle was helping me, whether I knew it or not, pointing out all the details I had missed.

After this, I knew I had committed myself to him.

Perhaps now is a good time to say that, as far as I know, these interviews are the only published documentation of Masha. For the eight years I knew him, Mayah kept him successfully tucked away from the media. When she was pointedly asked about her "adopted son," she gracefully sidestepped the questions by explaining that she didn't want her family members raised "under the heat of public scrutiny."

Usually, every few months, I'd hear a rumor about him ripple through the gossip pond—the identity of his father, how Mayah kept him hidden because of hideous deformities, etc.—but the stories were usually laughably inaccurate and no serious fan considered them. For the most part, the press kept a nice, civil distance from him.

Even I was only allowed glimpses. After the herbal tour, I didn't speak to Masha for over a year and a half, which began to make me anxious. Still not learning my lesson, I sent another request to Mayah for her permission to publish the talks. I offered her the option to redact any of the material she disliked, and then, just to encourage the process, I sent her the transcripts to read over.

No response.

So I gave up on doing anything professional with the talks, and I decided to put my energy toward my health. When the symptoms came on, I'd attack myself with a round of white, powdery supplements or aggressive bodywork, and watch the pain temporarily flee to some dark nook of myself. But it always seemed to return, burrowing back into my organs to feast on as much tissue as possible.

It's funny, in those rare moments when the symptoms entirely dissipated, I'd begin to question whether I'd exaggerated the whole situation. I was so eager to erase the reality of it from my memory that I'd take any opportunity I had to forget it ever happened.

Over time, these moments added up and I felt better slightly more often than I felt worse. I stopped identifying myself as "the sick person," and my friends stopped exclaiming, "You look so much better!" every time they saw me. If I forgot about it, so would everyone else.

But a few months before the following interview, I felt the early tickles of a flare-up. It always started at the base of my belly—a swelling. I had become obnoxiously sensitive to the subtle ways my immune system sputtered. A patch of eczema, a trapped bubble of air in my small intestine—these small pains would accrete over days until the sum of them became a storm that would confine me to my apartment for weeks.

At that particular moment, I wasn't in the storm yet, but I could see it coming, a few weather systems away. So, as a preventative measure, I took a few humiliating tests—shit in a bin, spit in a tube, piss in a cup—and I received a graph with a rising line and some gentle slopes. Supposedly, this was proof of bacterial overgrowth. The peaks were where my microbiome consumed sugar and produced gases. The troughs were where they died off. The hundred trillion bugs, viruses, and archaea in my gut, my microbial community, were in a state of social unrest. They'd begun letting in nasty organisms—with villainous names like enterobacter and klebsiella—and this situation, I was told, could be the source of all my troubles. My inner culture was out of balance.

Now, of course, nobody could say what *caused* the overgrowth, just that it was there, and had to be demolished with antibiotics, and rebuilt with probiotics. Sounded like a plan.

Around this time, Mayah launched *Turnstyle*, her new lifeway magazine. It covered all of the topics regularly featured on her network show: parenting, sex, diet, sleep, movement, psychology, recipes, music, and myths. It achieved quick, effortless popularity.

Several long-form think pieces were written about the magazine and the enormous media empire surrounding it, sometimes known as "Mayah's Queendom." Most of these described the untouchable social status she had carved out. This was a historically new kind of command for a woman to wield in American society, and the movers loved it.

Of course, some hated her for it, contemptuous of anyone who held power. Some criticized her endorsement of lying and amnesia, but the direction of the opinions didn't matter. Every calorie of interest boosted her higher and higher, until *Time* magazine agreed that she was the most influential person in the world. With a few cursory mentions, she could singlehandedly usher a nobody into the celebrity circle. If she spoke your name aloud, up went your sales, ratings, accolades, cachet. With this influence, she selectively promoted key figures around PM, choosing experts in scientific fields to validate the work, actors to promote it, and spiritual leaders to sanctify it. She opened the movement's access point as wide as culture itself so that every human being could be welcome.

The tabloids began a surveillance of Mayah's romances, which were frequent, fleeting, and bisexual. During the week of this interview, the entertainment news shows ran photos of Mayah exiting an acupuncture clinic in Miami with an unknown, scruffy male figure, the two of them hooded and in sunglasses, gripping each other's arms. A few weeks before that, she'd been spotted with fashion designer Claudia Rola-Smith on the red carpet at a charity gala. She was unabashedly public in her displays of affection. No one could take their eyes off her.

This was the moment when I finally received a phone call from Mayah. She had read the transcripts, she said, but felt that the time still wasn't right for their publication. I was disappointed and sighed audibly into the phone. As a snide response, I brought up the recent photos of her and asked for a comment. It was a childish attempt to get a reaction from her and I immediately regretted it. But she laughed me off with nonchalance and suggested that, if I was still interested, I should speak to Masha about some of his "problems."

"What problems?" I asked her

"Getting into *the life*," she said, which I assumed meant public life. "I know how much he enjoys speaking to you. Maybe one of your talks will help."

A week later, I passed through a series of security checkpoints and signed a waiver, consenting to be filmed while on the premises in *Mayah!* studios. I used the bathroom, as I always do before interviews, to clear my bowels of any burning distractions, and then followed a guard to Masha's dressing room.

He opened the door before I could knock.

"I know your rhythm," he said.

When I laid eyes on him, I jerked. He appeared to have aged significantly since I'd last seen him. The adolescent face changes, I know, but in this case the pacing seemed off. I'd always placed Masha in his teens, and yet, at that moment he exhibited all signs of adulthood: his button nose had expanded into a masculine pair of nostrils. His hair was long and coarse, tied up in a messy bun, a few loose strands trembling in the breeze of the air conditioning. His skin looked leathery, as if he had spent every day in the sun since I'd last met with him, and his tattoos had multiplied, with stained-glass imagery spreading across his forearms, hands, and fingers.

The room was a large, windowless box with hardwood floors, a steel kitchen, and an open shower with blue matte tiles. A savory odor hung in the air. On the counters, plates and bowls were stacked up like towers in a miniature city caked in food. Every wall was covered in murals, mostly of animals and physiological schematics, and in the center of the room was a canvas tent with an unmade downy comforter inside.

We said awkward hellos to each other, found seats, and engaged in some introductory small talk, mostly about my day, which is something I hadn't yet done with Masha. I noticed that he seemed more versed in the movement's philosophy as it was publicly represented, and newly aware that his own opinions might conflict with it.

His responses were more erratic and colloquial, his old speech patterns eroded by the force of standard American English. Before I began recording, he paused mid-sentence, stared blankly into his vanity mirror for a few spaced-out seconds, and applied some thick salve to his cheeks. Then, as if snapping out of a dream, he looked at me in the mirror and laughed.

"OK, let's start already," he said. "I almost forgot you were here."

We spoke for two hours, though the number of words in the interview suggest a much shorter period, as Masha's responses often included long plateaus of silence.

* * *

MASHA ISLE: *[rubs his face]*

INTERVIEWER: Giving yourself a little massage?

MI: Mm. *[rubs]* I need this right now. All these glows, you know? My face—I'm not even sure what I'm doing with it anymore. I'm talking to someone and I'm glowing and it's like I—I can't even . . . I can't focus on both at once . . . talk and glow. Talk, glow. Tsch. It's too much. Especially right here *[presses on cheekbones]* and here. *[points to lower jaw]* It's all cramped.

I: I've had that. TMJ.

MI: Right? Right? It's like I can't get my face back to relax. I think it's stuck. So, uh, if you don't mind I might not look at you much when we're talking today.

I: Sure, yeah. Of course.

MI: I know that's not really something I'm supposed to say, right? Mayah wouldn't be thrilled to hear me talking like this. It's bad knowledge for sure, but I'm tired and I don't want to act around you.

I: No, no, of course I appreciate that. And I'll keep my eyes on my notebook. I've got a bunch of questions written down here and I can just take notes while we talk.

MI: Oh, but I didn't mean to say that *you* can't look at *me*. Because you can, if it helps you. *[closes eyes, rubs them]*

I: Maybe you need glasses?

MI: Mm. I don't think so. It's these people Mayah brings to me—they all want such attention. I don't think I can give them what they want.

I: So you've been around a lot of people.

MI: It's—Mayah's so excited to introduce me to all the great personalities she's ever made. She wants me to see real p in action. So every day there's someone moving around the room, showing me how good they are. "Look at them thrive!" Mayah says to me. But I just can't be around them. I know I should *respect the holy personality* and I know I should love all the stories of their personalities. *[in loud booming voice] Jerry V., the man who never makes the same glow twice! Randi P., the woman who can convince you to say anything.*

I: How does she do that?

MI: I don't know! I can't pay attention. I'm supposed to love all this. To meet a great personality is the most important experience! "Hold your gaze," Mayah says. "That's how you make friends with p." But I can't. I'm not like that.

I: Last time we met—when was that? Three years ago? You were in that yurt, or whatever—it was at the PM seminars and it didn't seem like you were having these sorts of problems.

MI: I was perfect back then. No headaches. None of this eyelid flapping I have now. All these new things are hurting me. Everything is a first! Every personality. How many firsts must I endure? There's always another exciting new thing in the world! A new food, place, sound. I hate it. Look what happens. *[points at his face, grimaces]* I, uh—I'm sure all this whining sounds ridiculous to you, but—but that's OK, right? You're here to talk. All these other people—they're Mayah's friends, so what can I say to them? Some of these people are coming around every day, reporting back to Mayah, and I have to glow the whole time I'm around all of them, petting their p, showing off my personality, loving them all the time.

I: Why—

MI: And then there's Dr. Shaw. He's here every time I drop my pants! Snapping pictures, asking his favorite questions: *[in a pensive, low voice]* "What's the form? Consistency? Is it flowered at the edges? Does it have a tail? How'd you sense the shape as it crowned? Did you visualize it, like we talked about? Or did you just let it go? How long were you aware of it before your movement?"

I: Stool analysis.

MI: Oh yeah, and I put it in these—these glass jars, and we stare at it and talk about it until he's satisfied. And if I don't answer all his questions about it, Mayah thinks I'm disrespecting her. *[mimicking Mayah's voice]* "I didn't raise you to be like this."

I: What'd you call it before—*backstory*? I loved that.

MI: Oh yeah, tug talk.

I: And what exactly are you supposed to learn from this process?

MI: The idea is, the p might not make it past the gut, and then you've got it backed up inside you. It gets trapped in other places, such as your face. Like this. *[points at his face]* But that—Dr. Shaw—that's just first thing in the morn. Then it's lessons. Then it's hair and makeup. Then camera rehearsal. *[distracted]* Hey, wha—what's that? *[points at I's notebook to a taped image of Mayah and the mystery man, clipped from* US Weekly *magazine]*

I: Oh, I brought this to talk about. Do you know who this is? *[points at the man]*

MI: Yeah, of course, it's Polpy.

I: That's Polpy? That man she's with?

MI: Or no, I'm sorry I shouldn't have said that. It's *Messina.* That's bad knowledge on my part. Forget that, I'm sorry. Just use *Messina.* Don't tell Mayah I said that. She'd be fumed. Forget that. Erase it from your recorder.

I: Why?

MI: He's at the end of his turn. I can't be talking like that. He's still too open-minded.

I: About what?

MI: Calling him by that name. It could hurt him.

I: Polpy.

MI: That isn't even a word anymore. He's Messina all the time. Messina. Messina.

I: Even here in privacy.

MI: No. Best to forget. Why spread it? I should talk as if he were here. That's the most attractive way to be: act as if every human being is always nearby. Always listening and watching.

I: So all this rubbing and stress has nothing to do with your father?

MI: No, no. It's more like I was saying before: my body is hating all these personalities. I should be saving myself.

I: Because when we last spoke you hadn't been in touch with him since you left your childhood home. When did you last see him?

MI: When Mayah was trotting him around backstage. She introduced him to everyone as Messina, her perfect high school boyfriend who was now a professional photographer and who was taking a portrait of her.

I: Does he look the same?

MI: No. He shaved his beard. I'd only always seen him wearing his robe before and now he wears pants and shirts. And boots! So it took me a few moves before I knew it was him. He didn't even have his mole anymore. *[points to his cheek]* Used to be right here.

I: He had it removed?

MI: Or it just went away.

I: That takes years, though, right?

MI: Then I guess he removed it! I don't know. I shouldn't even be talking this way. Why talk like this? You keep tricking me into it.

I: Oh, I'm sorry. I don't mean to—I'm not sure . . .

MI: *[mashes down his nose, making the voice nasal in tone]* It's fine. Just keep asking, asking, asking.

I: Uh, we can stop if this is bothering you.

[silence]

MI: *[still mashing]* No, no, go. This is how it *has* to be. I've got to learn.

I: OK . . . um, I was curious, when you said your father and Mayah have known each other since they were in high school—have they really?

MI: I don't know.

I: You think it's a lie?

MI: That's Mayah's most hated word.

I: Right, I know, but—but what do *you* think?

MI: I don't know . . . Stop asking that. If he says they did, just believe it. You have to give people a chance. You can't always be pointing your finger and crying "liar" every time anyone wants to take a turn.

I: But either they dated in high school or they didn't, right?

MI: No.

I: No?

MI: No, I disagree.

I: How can you disagree with that?

MI: I'd rather let people say what they want. That's more important than they did or didn't. That kind of talk doesn't allow for any good, satisfying turns. You're blocking p.

I: You don't thinking lying is unethical?

MI: Of course not. Why would it be?

I: I guess, because it creates, you know, forking realities. You never know what's real. To me *that's* what gets confusing.

MI: Forking realities, he says! No, no. *That word* is what makes forking realities. It's meaningless. Everyone is so paranoid about being deceived. Who cares? Be deceived. Enjoy it.

I: What's that little adage you and Mayah like to say? "A lie is just a new idea before its time"?

MI: Mm. *[nods]*

I: But didn't you—I mean, I remember us talking before about your mother deceiving you and that really seemed to bother you.

MI: Bah. As a tug, maybe.

I: But you seemed so disturbed by it—the stuff about her—

MI: I also used to be smaller. I couldn't walk. I had other teeth. I refused to eat potatoes because I knew they were the heads of furry garden rodents. That's how I thought when I was a tug. I'm not like that anymore.

I: So, OK, why do you think most people are so upset by lying and trickery then?

MI: Because their personality's dead. It just sits there, too slow and heavy to move until it rots away. It wants everything to be the same all the time. It's a dead, stiff thing. But dead, stiff things break. Living things are soft and warm. They bend.

I: And lying is bending the truth.

MI: Not if you keep calling it that. You won't ever bend anything if you keep talking like that.

I: Have you been spending time with Messina?

MI: I tried. Mayah brought him in here and presented him to me. She posed him in front of me and kept giving me her funny little glows from over his shoulder.

I: She was showing him off.

MI: And she should have. It was a great first. Because I wasn't talking to Polpy, I was *meeting* Messina. He kept asking if I worked on the show and what my name was. "Are you Mayah's son?" Just like you did when you first met me.

I: He didn't recognize you?

MI: Oh no, no. He'd forgotten me very well, which is how I know how potent his personality was. Not a single unnecessary glow. Every movement happening at the right moment. Mayah was showing me exactly what it looks like to have enough power to wipe yourself out, which is exactly what I need right now.

I: To forget? *[silence]* But didn't you do something like that? You were talking about it last time, right?

MI: Not yet. I've been having too many problems recently.

I: It seems like the show's been pushing toward more intense amnesiac turns like that.

MI: It's not all about picking and choosing anymore. It's easier. No acting. She's just digging into the whole sack now. All or nothing.

I: Are you getting involved in the show? Is that why you're staying here?

MI: I'm just learning the tanks, steamers, hair, makeup. But I'm not allowed onstage yet. I still can't see p. Mayah's always trying to help me. She'll be working on someone and she'll wave me over and point out the way a certain organ glows, but I can never really see it. Like, she was making a turn backstage last night, and it was just us—the crew had all left—and she brought over her skin hammer to tap on one of the warmers—the one right here *[points to the tendon between the shoulder and the bicep]* and as she taps . . . taps . . . *[closes his eyes, taps in air]* this guy's face started immediately lighting up, and I could see her tuning him, right there. She'd tap wherever she wanted to glow. She tipped the head and let the p pool in the eye, and if she didn't like the way it glowed, she tipped it the other way. She was *sculpting* the personality right there. I'd seen her do this before, but this was the first time I watched her dial in *exactly* what she wanted. Perfectly. She could turn the face just enough to make you fall in love with him.

I: But you couldn't see any of his glows?

MI: No, I could see all that. That's easy. It's foreseeing that's hard. When Mayah chose that exact spot on the shoulder, she asked me where she should tap, and I just couldn't see it. I would have been guessing. And yet she saw it as bright as the sun. She can see a glow and *[waves his hand]* move it in a second. That's all she sees—glows floating everywhere. Not even people, just an ocean of light.

I: Is that what you'd like to see?

MI: Of course! That's what's going on all the time, and I'm missing it. All because I'm too busy smelling my breath getting worse every day. *[makes a gagging face]* Old rotten p filling me up. Messina could even smell it too. I saw him wince.

I: Is he helping with making turns too? Is the whole family involved?

MI: No, no. He's not made like that. He likes to give other people attention. He doesn't like to get too much.

I: Is that how he's different?

MI: What do you mean *how*?

I: Like, uh, we talked about the walking before—remember? You looked at my gait and told me all the aspects that were wrong about it, which seemed like everything.

MI: I didn't say that.

I: No *[laughs]* you're right. You said I had too much p in it, which I've actually thought a lot about. I spent a while looking at myself in the mirror while stepping . . .

MI: Which isn't helpful . . .

I: But, I guess what I'm asking is—for example, Messina's walk, is it radically different than it was before? I'm just trying to picture—

MI: Here I'll just show you. *[stands, pauses, walks slowly]* You see that?

I: Uh—

MI: Watch. *[walks back and forth]*

I: The knee?

MI: No, no. The foot. On the back end of the step. *[taps the leg]*

I: How it drags like that?

MI: Yeah. That's good. You're seeing it. *[swings foot back and forth]* That's one of Messina's moves. It's perfect, right? I've been going over it. *[dances feet back and forth]* And then there's that little scoop at the end of it? See that? His moves don't always happen when you think they would. Just a little later, a little unexpected. And it's exactly what *makes* his personality, the way it changes your attention.

I: So, but what about . . . besides these physical things. How would you describe him in a nonphysical way?

MI: What do you mean?

I: His traits. How he is. Would you say Messina is smart or kind or grumpy or whatever, whereas before he was—

MI: Aw, come on, don't talk like that.

I: What do you mean?

MI: I hate that talk. Makes it hard to love you when I hear that out of your mouth. All that stuff is garbage. Terrible knowledge. There's no chance you'll ever feel your p calling everyone names. She's carefree! He's a downer! I don't want to talk like that. Nobody is grumpy or smart. They only move that way.

I: There's no such thing as a smart person?

MI: No. They only look that way.

I: So it's all in the moves?

MI: It's the body, yes. Personality is right here. *[shakes his hand in the air]*

I: So like, if someone has deep forehead wrinkles, that means they're a worrywart? Like that?

MI: I have no idea what you're talking about.

I: Well, like on the show—

MI: I can't talk about that.

I: Have you stopped watching it?

MI: Oh, no. Of course not. I sneak it all the time. Check this out. *[unzips the tent and reveals a silver, cordless portable television set hidden beneath a blanket]*

I: Is Mayah OK with you watching now?

MI: Not really, no. But I do it anyway and she knows and that's how it will always be. I know it's ruining me, but I love it.

I: Does she watch television herself?

MI: No.

I: Doesn't that seem hypocritical?

MI: Who cares. She is a source of p for people everywhere. Look what she can do. She just made her most joyous work yet. Messina. Completely genuine and real. There isn't a second of acting in him anywhere. I don't know how to say it better than that. Just watch the episode. You'll see.

I: Oh yeah. So he's in next season?

MI: Of course, yes, yes, he's always with cameras, three, four of 'em, day and night. He hates them, but he loves his new personality, so he does it.

I: And how do you know he isn't just faking it? I mean this is something I've been wondering for a while. Like who was the guy who came out recently and admitted that he had never really taken a turn? That he'd just been pretending to be how he thought he *should* be. He wasn't a different personality at all. He didn't feel anything different.

MI: Where was that?

I: It was—he was always on Donel.

MI: Don't watch that crap.

I: *[laughs]*

MI: That just wouldn't happen with Mayah. She'd be able to see it. That guy, the one you're talking about, he gave up, right? He couldn't keep it going. That's because acting takes effort. Turning doesn't. That feeling, when the greatest actor performs every word like reality—that can't last forever. The greatest actor alive couldn't do that forever. The acting would eventually rip her apart, all the p would spill out, and then she'd get sicker and sicker and die. But with a turn, if you keep up the basic exercises, you can keep the p healthy and circulating. Anyone could do it. The weakest man alive. It's not acting. It's about being totally sincere and transparent. *[rubbing his eyes, opening his mouth widely, sticking out his tongue]*

I: But what about that man in the last season—the one who got a repetitive stress injury from the foot exercises?

MI: Trying hard is pretty much the worst thing for new p. But everyone does it. I don't know why, but everyone here, all they know how to do is work themselves. But p doesn't need to be forced. Once Mayah opens it up, there's nothing to do but let it flow. Just give it a gentle direction. That's just—

I: You called my p gentle.

MI: I did?

I: Yeah, actually, a few years back. I always wondered what that meant and—

MI: *[rests head on the vanity table, lets out a long "ah" sound]*

[both MI *and* I *remain quiet for several moments]*

I: Are you OK?

MI: Yes, no. I am.

I: It's fine if you aren't. Be honest. Should we stop?

MI: You know, yeah, that would be good. I think I'm just feeling a little full.

V.

March 2002

BURBANK, CA

Publicly, Marshal Isle was born on the premiere episode of season 16. Mayah sent me a ticket for the show and I attended the live taping in Burbank, a short drive from the Los Feliz neighborhood of Los Angeles where I was then living.

I arrived excited to see the new stage, which had been dramatically remodeled, from the traditional couch-and-desk set of most talk shows into an open-faced, two-story house design. I sketched out a quick diagram of the scene in my notebook. I described each room's distinct character, expressed with wallpapers, flooring, decorations, and fetish objects. A recent article in *Turnstyle* had explained how each room would be used for different kinds of guests. The violet and yellow room, for example, featured a dreamy soundtrack, a bergamot scent, and some moody lighting gels—a kind of bedroom setting for guests who were having trouble with what Mayah called "staying in the waking state."

The audience that day expressed the show's usual demographic: primarily women, with a light sprinkling of men (most of whom were probably accompanying women) and a variety of international supporters. On my right, an older Filipino-American mother and her middle-aged daughter spoke in their native tongue; on my left, an Irish lady, who had flown in from Dublin for the show, read a thin biography of Amelia Earhart.

As show time approached, the stage manager instructed us to applaud when the signs flashed. The house band fired up the show's triumphant theme song and the crowd stomped their feet. An older couple stood up and danced in the aisles.

When the music faded, Mayah trotted onstage and in her big round bell of a voice, bellowed the standard opening call:

"Whaaaaaaat?"

And then, as usual, she waited with open arms for the audience to reply:

"Nooooooow!"

She then gave a long, poetic monologue on "the ocean of p," which included some of her favorite topics—mitochondria, weight loss, spring hats—before building to her big announcement.

"Now that I have a new home," she said, pointing to the new stage, "I guess I need a family to put in it, don't I?"

The crowd hooted, the lights dimmed, and she made a theatrical disappearance behind the big red curtains. Smoke bloomed from beneath the floorboards and the house band thrummed a drone as images of young, ruddy boys flashed on a screen above the stage. When Mayah returned, she led a blindfolded man to the center of the stage, her face beaming, her eyes moistened with tears—close-ups caught all the details. Then an explosive crack from a snare drum, a spotlight, and Mayah removed the scarf to reveal her new cohost.

The young man wore a white kilt that hung to his knees. Atop his head, a firm-looking dome of a haircut. A sleeveless terrycloth vest clung to his chest. His limbs were carved caramel.

The crowd erupted at the sight of him and he absorbed their reaction, smiling with an ease that I spent a long time admiring before I fully realized the remarkable, ineffable transformation that had taken place. No bundle of descriptors can truly convey the uncanny experience of staring with pure wonder at someone with whom you are already intimately familiar. You struggle to *see* him, not because of blurred vision, but because any possibility of recognition had been anticipated and deflected with expertise.

Mayah announced the man as her son, Marshal, and led him through the audience, up and down the aisles, close enough to allow every individual to lay their hands upon him. She called this "being somatically introduced" and he nodded and giggled through the whole process, taking it all in like a prize winner basking in acceptance.

On the screen above us, a short film displayed Marshal creeping into a low-ceilinged basement—PM fans later called this the "doghouse." The video depicted Mayah spoon-feeding Marshal with what she told the camera was "the Belladonna fast." She demonstrated how to mash thornapple into a honey-infused oil that could be used, in trace amounts, in basic cooking. She explained that during the two-week fast, Marshal sat almost completely still and was only allowed to move in prescribed ways at specific times, a procedure that would help him detoxify from his old personality.

As uncomfortable as the video looked, Marshal seemed to skip through every scene like an appreciative puppy. At the end, after a long time-lapse shot, he emerged from the basement, naked and wide-eyed, squinting at the sky. The camera held a long shot of his face, which had become remarkably chiseled since I last saw him, and the music thrashed to a climax. All of it felt a bit heavy-handed for my taste, but the women flanking me seemed genuinely overwhelmed with emotion.

The rest of the episode took the form of a one-on-one conversation. Marshal described how he could "feel the world on his skin . . . like a baby!" and thanked Mayah repeatedly. I noticed that he spoke at a slightly lower pitch than Masha, and that he produced words with a satisfying new click and pop, as if every syllable were cut from wood and stone.

At one point, he sprinted through the house set, jumped onto a bed, stamped his feet, and did a kind of twist-flip in time with the band's soaring R&B melody. A woman called out for his hand in marriage. Later, a Norwegian teenage girl crawled onstage, threw her arms around him, and fell into some kind of ecstatic fit.

The episode was the most-watched television event of the month. The critical response, however, was polarized. Some of the more aggressive reviews denounced Marshal's "character game" as a publicity hoax. Others worried that it was not a hoax, that Mayah's ascetic practices had led her to what *The New York Times* called "torture TV" and "self-help without limits." The *New York Post* put the image of a fist-pumping Marshal on its cover, and in a bold, screaming font above it, the phrase "I'm ready!", an exclamation he'd made many times over the course of the episode. The *Chicago Tribune* called him "Mayah's new manservant."

Many saw the addition of a cohost as a lure to draw a younger audience to the movement. This was partly due to Marshal's activities outside the show, his lectures at colleges, where he would screen clips of the show that were unfit for network television (nudity, language, general intensity) and give advice for at-home personality work. The events were overwhelmingly popular.

On a trip to New York shortly before the following interview, I attended one of Marshal's two sold-out lectures at the New School's Tishman Auditorium in Manhattan. Onstage, he carried himself with the sort of gliding confidence I would have once described as natural. He danced on the balls of his feet, as if his enthusiasm for the material was inflating him with kinetic energy. He pulled audience members onstage and bantered with a wry humor that wouldn't have suited Mayah, but somehow perfectly complemented her ideas. He sang, made goofy faces. He oozed charisma and the crowd loved him for it. I loved him for it. How could I not? Here was a person *made* to be the object of adoration. You could feel it.

For my purposes, I would go as far as saying it's the responsibility of any subject to *help* their interviewer adore him, to *make* me respond to his every phrase with a desire to know more. If the interviewee does their job, my questions should spill out of me in a stream of endless curiosity: And then what? And then what? They give me curiosity, and in return, I give them attention, and therefore, love.

To clarify, I'm using *love* as Isle used it. I loved his *personality*. I wanted to walk through the world as if I were living inside him, and he inside of me. I didn't want to seduce him or marry him, I just wanted to believe in him.

In fact, this "love" may have been the first time I ever believed in anything. For most of my adult life, I didn't find the nonmaterial world worthy of attention—spirits, faeries, gods, emotions of uncertain origin. I told myself that I was happy with the world as it simply appeared to be. And I must say, that perspective held strong for a long time, right up until my body collapsed on itself.

I imagine that all biographers must experience a least a whiff of this infatuation. Did Eckhart feel it for Goethe? Boswell for Johnson? Plato for Socrates? I think so. What other kind of energy could fuel such a long-term, seemingly selfless project as chronicling another person's life? What is that, if not love?

I've often had to defend my enthusiasm for PM. For years I was an apologist, always on the defensive with friends and editors, breathlessly trying to justify the movement and my interest in it. Almost everyone I knew scoffed at the extremist methods and the horrors of the celebrity culture that surrounded it—two critiques which were pretty hard to refute. I'm usually pretty good in a hot debate, but those days I felt like a bigot with a stammer: I was perpetually searching for the perfect explanation for what my friends dismissed as an immature fixation. But eventually, I just stopped caring. To hell with them. I was high on intuition.

As I saw it, Marshal addressed the criticisms of PM through his very being. How could PM be nothing more than escapism, as many people said, when this man had not only rejected a former self, but truly inhabited a new, shining personality? This man gave me a model. All I saw in Marshal, as he projected his voice from the stage, was a human exactly as he should be, and I wanted to celebrate him for it.

After the lecture, I waited and watched him take on a queue of fans that wrapped around the block. He generously spoke with each person, touching their shoulders, snickering at their jokes, and radiating his endless supply of sunny extroversion. I stuck around over an hour for a chance to congratulate him—to *meet* him, really—but ultimately, I didn't want to meet him that way. It wouldn't be right. I wasn't just another fan.

A few weeks later, Shara Ulman, Mayah's new publicist, called and asked if I would like to interview Marshal for an upcoming issue of *Turnstyle.* "He's looking forward to meeting you," she said, before launching into a list of topics I should avoid during the interview—classic PR micromanaging.

This was a peculiar time for me, career-wise. I seemed to have acquired some momentum from years of bylines in reputable publications, and yet I didn't know where I was headed. I spent a lot of my time surrounded by famous, seemingly compelling individuals, but I had lost my fascination for the work itself. Over the last decade I'd been keeping my head down, literally navel-gazing, tracking my health in ten-minute intervals, consumed with myself to the exclusion of all else. Years later, when I finally looked up, I found myself inhabiting the career of a talking head.

A few times a month I'd get requests, usually by news outlets, to comment on some cultural happening, and I'd spend a few hours scrambling to construct a perspective that seemed sturdy enough to present as my own. How did I feel about the legacy of some recently deceased so-and-so actress? What does her death say about the lineage of all women in film? Of women in society? How was cinema changed by her presence? Did I enjoy her final performance in the acclaimed dramedy about important such-and-such social issue of the moment? And on and on.

My talk with Isle, I hoped, could be a departure from the news cycle I'd been caught in. Over the course of our last four meetings, I'd increasingly felt like I was in the presence of a friend, and I hoped that this dynamic hadn't been entirely lost in the turn.

The interview took place at Ulman's Santa Monica office during the show's off-season. Marshal was scheduled for a string of interviews that afternoon, and mine would be sandwiched between *People* and *Time.*

On my arrival, Ulman showed me to an empty conference room where I set up my new digital recorder, which I tested three times to ensure it was working correctly, since, unlike my old one, it was always completely silent.

When she returned with Marshal, I broke into a quick sweat. He removed his sunglasses and strode toward me with a wide, earnest grin, remarking how nice it was to "finally meet me," as if dozens of people had mentioned my name to him. I laughed in agreement and I remember feeling uncertain about how to physically position myself in relation to him. I thought of Amazonian cultures, deep in the forest, who purposely forgot those who died. They burned the belongings of the dead and never again invoked their names so that the souls of the deceased could travel to the beyond without burdens from the physical world.

Up close, I could see the deep color of his hale complexion and the power of his chin, which seemed more prominent now, as if it were leading the rest of him. As we began talking, his eyes rested on my face and remained there for the next hour, giving me a feeling that was initially unnerving—nauseating, even—but then, over the course of our interview became so comforting that I missed the quality in everyone else I encountered over the next few days.

The transcript that follows was published in a highly abridged version in *Turnstyle.* It came out during the ratings blitz known as "sweeps week."

* * *

INTERVIEWER: I hear you're coming from another interview.

MARSHAL ISLE: Yep, just down the hall. Ended a few minutes ago. And you? Where are you coming from?

I: Oh, just the east side.

MI: You live over there?

I: Yes, for a few years now, with a roommate I met online.

MI: Living with a stranger.

I: Once a stranger. Now a person who knows the most intimate details of my life.

MI: Oh yes. So true. I love that.

I: And so this interview you're coming from—what'd you talk about there? I don't want to ask you all the same questions you've been answering all day.

MI: I'm sure you won't, but, if you'd like to know, the last couple of questions were about the kind of product I used in my hair and what type of women I find attractive. *[laughs]*

I: How'd you answer?

MI: Truthfully, I have no idea what product goes in my hair. It's all chosen by Gina[1] and I'm thankful I don't have to consider it.

---

[1] Regina Yang, Marshal's in-house stylist.

I: And the women?

MI: I find all of them attractive.

I: All women?

MI: No, all types of women. That was the question.

I: Sounds like a cop-out.

MI: No, no. That's an authentic answer.

I: So you're saying you have absolutely no preference toward any type of women? What about the ones with drool leaking from their mouths and hateful ideas running through their heads?

MI: Yes, those! *[laughs]* I like them too.

I: Do you find all these interviews exhausting?

MI: *[shakes head]* Not at all. I enjoy it. I'm energized, actually.

I: Because when we spoke last time you were having difficulty.

MI: I'm sure that's true but—

I: But you don't remember any of that.

MI: No, I don't.

I: None of it.

MI: No.

I: And of course you also don't remember anything about me . . .

MI: I was told that we've spoken before, but no, I don't have *memories* of it.

I: *[laughs]* Really? I know we shouldn't linger on this, but—

MI: I totally understand if my presence is making you uncomfortable.

I: No, well, I guess I just didn't realize that this would be so . . . I mean, it's very hard to appreciate this situation if you haven't gone through it before.

MI: Yes, many people feel that way.

I: When you watch it on screen, on the show, it's one thing. Or even when I was in the audience and you were onstage—even then, it still seemed like performance, and I imagined that underneath, you were still the same as before.

MI: Right.

I: But I guess that's just what you think when there's a stage—it's all for show.

MI: I can certainly see how it might seem that way. Do you feel that I'm only acting this way?

I: No, no. You wouldn't do that, I know. It's just, even though I knew what was going to happen, and I spoke to Mayah about it, I guess it didn't sink in.

MI: Right.

I: And you really don't remember any of our prior meetings at all?

I: No, I try not to.

I: You try? See, now—what's that? Because if you're *trying*, that sounds like you haven't forgotten. That sounds like acting. That's what you told me, before.

MI: I'm always trying, even if I would rather not be. I can't help it. Neither can you. It's funny, there's this impression people have about taking a turn: that it's instantaneous, that forgetting your memories is as easy as pouring water from a cup. You just say goodbye to them forever. But it's not as clear as that. It's not done with brute force. The effort is more feminine. Sinuous. It's not work, but an ongoing negotiation with memory. Different every day. Always dynamic. This is the same kind of relationship you have with your personality. If you can speak with it, then maybe you can recognize the distance between it and you. Then you can love it.

I: So it's not like amnesia. One second and your whole history is erased.

MI: No, no. You ease into it. You need a soft mind to truly forget. No memory is really gone until you want it gone. Not once. Not twice. Every day. You're always paddling out of the current.

I: I'm not sure I know what that would be like, to want some memory out of my head with such vehemence.

MI: Ah, but you do. You forget all day long. You may not do it on purpose but you are always selecting memories to trim and others to carry with you, everywhere you go. It's no different. I'm just paying attention to it.

I: Mayah thinks we're too obsessed with our memories, right? If you love something, set it free.

MI: Memory is not who we are.

I: So then, in your case, are your memories lost forever? Or are they just more distant from your daily thoughts?

MI: For me, I'd have to spend a lot of time and effort to return to them. I've made sure of that. The process is not dissimilar from recalling a dream. If you try to keep it, maybe it remains for a few hours. Maybe you maintain a connection with it for weeks. Maybe you write down one special dream and read it over from time to time, and perhaps you occasionally recall a fleeting moment of it. But for the most part, you forget your dream easily. Just like that. It isn't useful to your life, so why keep it? But if you want to try and recall a random dream from two years ago—really, truly remember it, the details and everything—that's almost impossible. And that's how life memories are too. Just let them float away.

I: At the lecture last month, you talked about "underworld dreaming." What is that?

MI: Dreams are one of the rare times you can forget about personality, and if you pay attention, you can truly feel fresh new p circulating through you, replenishing itself while you sleep. It's one of the greatest sensations in life. I often talk about this in my lectures to students because they can still get high from their dreams. That language still makes sense to them. In dreams, p flows in every direction. It's in the air. It's not confined to our bodies. You can move through it. You can feel it holding you up.

I: And what happens to our personality then, when we're sleeping?

MI: You aren't making it. You're resting that part of yourself. I'm sure you know the feeling, yes?

I: I remember when I was a kid I used to have lucid dreams all the time and at some point I discovered that in the dream world your hands aren't your own. If you look at them they could be anything—monkey hands, a baby's hands—and even then, they don't even stay the same. They keep changing throughout the dream. Every time you look at them, it's a different pair of hands. It's the same way your dream wife isn't always your real wife and your dream friends aren't always your real friends.

MI: And your dream memories aren't your real memories.

I: OK, but I still don't understand how someone *tries* to forget. That seems like a paradox.

MI: What if I called it "not remembering"? You don't have to forget, you can just *not* remember. Just don't try to remember. Is that better for you?

I: Hm. Yeah. I—

MI: It's all about where you put attention. When we're up at Peggy Creek [Hot Springs[2]] if a guest begins to misremember I'll simply encourage them to *turn attention toward p.* That's how we say it. And that's all you need to do.

I: Every day?

MI: Throughout your life, yes. And how we keep it up is through our five by fives: five senses, five minutes, five times a

---

[2] The mountain resort-spa in the San Gabriel Mountains where Mayah's guests stay during turns.

day—always turning toward p. Touch, hear, see, smell, taste—in that order. But this doesn't help anyone forget, it just helps you to fall in love with new memories.

I: It's that simple.

MI: Not simple at all. I have trouble with it every day. So does Mayah. We all do. Because there's always a new situation. Does the flavor of watermelon affect p? Does the sound of your neighbor's voice? Does the feel of a cotton sleeve rubbing against your wrist?

I: These all seem like unanswerable questions, right?

MI: No, I don't think so. They each require their own sensitivity. And sometimes I have to run through all my senses and every one of my expressions in the mirror just to feel stabilized. To see my glow. And I do it until I get the shiver.

I: I've heard of the shiver, but I've never felt it.

MI: Runs from the psoas to the vagus to the pituitary. *[draws a finger up the center of his body]* When you feel it, all the effort seems like a small price to pay. People, they don't know what they're missing. They're just getting tossed around by their personality. But once you feel the kind of stability I'm talking about, once you feel like you're meeting your personality with confidence, that's when you can start to live.

I: And you do this exercise every day? What happens if you don't?

MI: If you miss a session the memory gets messy. Miss two and memories blur. And from there it's increasingly difficult to sort out new memories from old ones.

I: You have to be strict.

MI: Just regular. But it's easy if you want it to be. You can do the work anywhere—on a bus, in the bathroom, in a parade. I do it mid-conversation.

I: Right now!

MI: Always.

I: I mean, essentially the only time we naturally lose memory is from a violent blow to the head, right? Or a degenerative disease. I think that's why some people have questioned the emphasis on forgetting in the last season. It just has such negative associations—illness, violence, aging.

MI: I think you're right and I think we even have that problem with guests. They're hesitant. Last season, the ones who didn't make it through the program—almost all of those cases were due to uncertainty: *Am I making the wrong decision?* And then what happens is they leave the spa, they stop their five by fives, and then, naturally, they stop holding. The ones who weren't hesitant were usually people who wanted to get rid of damaging memories. But that can be problematic too. They can be too eager.

I: But I'd imagine everyone has at least a little fear about such an enormous life choice.

MI: A little fear is good. It activates the sympathetic nervous system, and as soon as that happens you can see p light up all over. Jaw clenches—I always see that one. Then the peristaltic muscles spasm—little gurgles in the tummy. But when the indecision becomes distracting, then new p mixes with old p, which becomes very uncomfortable very quickly for the turn and their family. Maintenance is everything. Maintenance *is* personality. And vice versa. The problem is that most people want the quick fix.

I: Have you had any problems with your personality at all?

MI: I've been holding well so far. But I'm spoiled—I have the entire crew and the spa available to me all the time.

I: And what happens if you just stop the sessions altogether?

MI: It's different for everyone. Some thrive no matter what.

I: For example?

MI: I'd rather not discuss that.

I: Why not?

MI: Well, the more we talk about it the more real that possibility becomes. I'd rather that our guests didn't point their attention in the direction of failure. I'd rather we don't put those ideas into the airwaves.

I: So you never discuss the negative repercussions?

MI: No, not me. I don't want that talk out of my mouth. People can get that from the rest of the world. There's plenty of it around.

I: Seems like community is crucial to making a successful turn.

MI: For sure. We have eighteen employees dedicated exclusively to community support. Your family *has* to be involved, and usually they are, because they know, intimately, why the turn had to be made in the first place. They were there before the turn. They know what bad p can feel like. And so they're often the ones who contact us. We appreciate it when family members nominate each other, for whatever reason. Maybe problems have arisen at home. Maybe they've already tried psychotherapy or drug rehabilitation and that didn't work out. So they come to us. In those cases the families are very helpful, from the intervention to the followthrough.

I: Everything has to be so fastidious and controlled for a turn to succeed.

MI: But consider what we're working against. A history of polluted personality. A lifetime of being numbed to the p that's all around us. Is that natural?

I: Who do you think is numbing us?

MI: Just culture. *[waves his hands around]* All of it. Everything. It's nobody in particular. It's just the nature of society. You can't be too sensitive around here. *[laughs]*

I: Do you think everyone should take a turn?

MI: I don't make statements like that, but I would hope most people get to truly feel p at some point in life. It would be a shame to miss out on that. I don't even care how they do it, turn or not. Use any method you like. But it's as fundamental as anything—food, sleep, shelter, family, personality.

I: In regards to family, I'm thinking of the Martin Mario episode[3] and how his wife brought him in . . .

---

[3] "The Forty-Five-Year-Old Infant," Aired: 11/1/01

MI: And that's a case where Mario—he's as steadfast as it gets. He's a house painter, and he often does his p work while he's painting. And he's wonderfully sensitive. He smells the latex. He feels the rollers he uses, how they react when he puts pressure on them. He's made these daily senses important to him. He wasn't always this way, though. At first, right after he took his turn, his wife used to have to bribe him with sex to get him to do the five by fives. But now he does it on his own because he recognizes himself better when he does. He's got this whole morning routine when he brushes his teeth and if he notices something off with his personality, he'll reach into his mouth and rub it out. He'll just take care of it right there. That's his trigger spot.

I: I heard him call you his "savior" in an interview.

MI: He saved himself.

I: No need for false modesty here.

MI: Maybe I just don't want that kind of responsibility.

I: Do you only deal with guests who are suffering?

MI: Yes, that's what we do.

I: You don't make cosmetic turns. Like, say, how Donel does.

MI: No.

I: And these family members who are bringing people to you, are they bringing people against their will? Like with Mario. His wife really instigated that, right? He didn't want to. She was threatening him with divorce.

MI: Yes.

I: Or like what about the Broderick episodes. [3/15/01–6/03/01] That was a tricky situation.[4] I was rewatching those shows and—

MI: Long before my time.

I: As far as I know, Broderick wasn't interested in the program or even generally in PM, and Mayah really had to coax her into participation, right?

MI: Yes.

I: Now see, she didn't seem like a person who was suffering. She seemed sort of OK with her decision. There's that photograph of her in the courtroom, smiling and raising her hand in an oath, which, I think that's how most people think about her. Wearing that smug grin. Pleased with herself. And I heard Broderick actually *disliked* the movement.

MI: Yes, that's an important point. Glad you brought it up. I think you're right. She felt justified. But you're suggesting that people always know when they need help, and I don't think that's true.

I: So who does know? Mayah?

MI: Yes, sometimes doctors, but in that case, it was the state. She was refusing to take part in the other prison therapy pro-

---

[4] Stacey Broderick was arrested for manslaughter after intentionally steering her Dodge minivan at the mistress of her husband [William "Billy" Broderick], breaking several of the woman's bones and putting her in a coma. Mayah worked with Broderick in prison for several months, filming weekly visits as part of an outreach program.

grams, and PM was her last option before she was placed in some kind of a solitary confinement situation.

I: So, would you say, in that particular instance, you worked with her against her will?

MI: No, no. She came around.

I: But, come on, like you're saying, what other choice did she have? Or more importantly, do you think that she really needed this turn? This kind of transformation? I mean, cheating on your wife is terrible, and her husband was certainly not in the right. But still, maybe she didn't need personality work.

MI: You feel this way? That violence like this is justified?

I: No, not me. I'm just playing the devil's advocate. I'm just trying to get at—

MI: I understand what you're asking and I know you want me to say something controversial like "She needed new p whether she wanted it or not." But I don't think that way and Mayah doesn't either. If Broderick didn't want to take the turn, it wouldn't have happened. She has to keep up the five by fives. We can't make her do that.

I: And she did.

MI: Oh yes. Once she experienced the smallest turn, she became very active in the movement. And now she's holding quite well.

I: And what about your turn—

MI: Mine was a full, hard turn.

I: Harder than most?

MI: Hard for me, but that was the only way I could take it.

I: Why's that?

MI: Well, because of situations like this interview, which require a certain flow of p. I had to be able to maintain that.

I: Which Masha didn't have.

MI: *[nods]*

I: I think that's true. Masha couldn't do this—what you're doing. He was too sensitive. Plus I don't think he even wanted to.

MI: The way you talk about him it sounds like you had some affection for him?

I: I did, yeah. I always walked away from our talks feeling . . . curious.

MI: Good, that's good.

I: But it sounds like you're satisfied with how things are.

MI: Oh yes, I have a completely fulfilling relationship with my personality now.

I: I read somewhere, some study that said 80 percent of our energy is spent on our personality.

MI: Only if you're wasteful. I hope I never leak energy like that. But is that how it feels to you? 80 percent?

I: Hm. I guess I'm not sure. I haven't really thought it through for myself.

MI: I'll give you a moment, if you want to think about it.

I: *[pauses]* Yeah, even right now I can definitely feel myself dumping a lot of energy into my personality. Maybe even more than 80 percent.

MI: Could be.

[both laugh]

I: What's the first memory you have as Marshal?

MI: Mayah's voice. For sure. When I was on my way out of the turn, her voice started to sing in the background. It was like a rope of words pulling me out of silence. It's one of those memories that I fall in love with every day. I think a lot of guests who come through here would probably tell you the same thing.

I: It's funny, I never hear people mention it, but of course, Mayah got her start in radio. Her golden voice was actually the first thing that got her an audience, right?

MI: Mm. There's so much in it. She's a great lover of the human voice. That's why she always addresses the guest's voice. It's the foundation for her.

I: Speaking of which—your voice, it's changed. I noticed it when I saw you onstage. It's like you have a different throat now. Your words are so thick and—

MI: Is it OK if I stop you there?

I: Sure—

MI: It's just, I don't want to step into too many physical memories . . . It's not as if I don't enjoy hearing it, but we've already been talking a bit too much in this direction, using his name, and—

I: Sorry, I'll stop.

MI: Just being responsible. I'm still sensitive. These descriptions are like little seeds that get fertilized in your mind and keep growing.

I: OK, so to keep going on your first memory: Where were you when you were hearing her voice?

MI: On a soundstage. But of course, I didn't know that at the time. I didn't know anything really.

I: It's that brightly colored stage, right? With the koi pond and plants and vines and rocks.

MI: Yep.

I: Was it just Mayah and you?

MI: No. People were passing through, checking on me. They're all pros. If they do their job right, they just disappear. I didn't even notice them.

I: I get the sense that Mayah's pretty fastidious when it comes to her staff.

MI: Oh yeah. All of them know how to keep as dim as possible.

Because at that point, when you're lying there in the tub, when you've just come out of it, you're hungry enough to eat up personality from anyone.

I: And so for you, what did it feel like at that point?

MI: During those first few days it was bodywork all the time. Especially the area around your mouth and eyes. Just getting a feel for all the simple things again, drawing p back into all these parts, building your face from the inside out. I spent a while at Peggy Creek. Longer than most. I had to pass eight goddamn golden nuggets from my liver!

I: And what was the first thing you did as a part of the show?

MI: Choosing the fall lineup—our guests—with Mayah.

I: I read that big piece in *Turnstyle* a few months back where she walked through the whole application process for guests. The first step is looking over the video, right? And it got me curious: What are you looking for when you watch a video?

MI: Receptivity. Does an applicant seems like she'll respond to our treatment? You can tell this through movement, definitely, but what I'm always listening for are what we call "pillows." Are they putting pillows into their speech? Softening it. Are they saying "probably" and "well" in every other phrase? Do they avoid making definitive statements? That's a way of watering down p, usually on purpose.

I: So once you decide, then what? Prep work?

MI: Yep. We'll usually start off with a basic time exercise.

I: Can you walk me through it?

MI: Sure. So to start, stand in place, eyes closed, without moving, and try to decide when a minute has passed. That's all. And no counting. That defeats the purpose. Then check the clock when you're ready and compare the real time with your own sense of time. Then try two minutes. Then five. Then an hour. Don't try to get more accurate with it. The point is to understand *your* time, not SI [Standard International] time.

I: What's this do?

MI: You'll learn a lot about your personality this way. All p moves through the body at different rates and if you're going to take a turn, you should have a well-developed time-telling muscle.

I: So, if I did this exercise every day, it would help me to take a turn?

MI: Maybe. Is that something you'd like to do?

I: I don't know. Not right now. *[notices Ulman motioning to her watch through the window]* Oh, hey, speaking of which, looks like we should be finishing up here. I think Shara just gave me the signal.

MI: Oh, yes. I have another interview coming up in a minute. I'd wanted to get in a short rest before it began, but that doesn't seems like it's going to happen.

I: Busy man. Sorry to have kept you.

MI: No need to apologize. I'm an adult. I could've stopped whenever I wanted to.

VI.

January 2004

NEW YORK, NY

In the months following Marshal's debut, the press swiftly adopted him as Mayah's rightful heir. He became a regular cover subject for the various cologne-soaked men's magazines—I counted six major profiles written on him in 2003 alone—and his appearance on the cover of *Rolling Stone*, with an ethnic rainbow of female hands stroking his face, became an iconic poster image of the early 2000s. An army of cliché-spouting journalists declared him "the spirit of his generation" and he wore the title proudly. Of all demographics, angsty teenage girls seem most immediately drawn to him, and I personally witnessed several of them dissolving into tears at his presence. His personal life also became a conspicuous affair. His casual dating of multiple international fashion models became standard entertainment news fodder, especially his mercurial relationship with the Lithuanian lingerie model Audrey Zelana.

The steep rise of his fame provided Marshal enough freedom to quickly introduce a wave of new techniques to the show. Many of these were controversial, and decidedly more aggressive than Mayah's talk-based approach. Some methods involved rough handling of guests, shaking their limbs and chanting at them in ways that made you want to both laugh and gasp. Others involved sexual rituals, shame induction, and increasingly radical forgetting. When he did use dialogue as a form of turning, the tone was blistering and interrogative, not the subtle suggestions of Masha. He'd repeatedly ask the same invasive questions of guests, forcing them to give different answers each time.

And yet, even in the most seemingly abrasive episodes, guests reported positive experiences and satisfying results. Audiences seemed to enjoy the high drama of Marshal's turns, which alternated weekly with Mayah's, giving a new balance of age, gender, and character to the show.

In late 2003, some movers began calling Marshal "the miracle worker," a claim that provoked prickly responses from religious types. But it was undeniable that the show had become a destination for anyone needing help—medical, emotional, or otherwise—and that Marshal seemed to tend to his guests in ways that Mayah had not. Yet he was always the first to admit that he could not cure disease, and to deny any intimation of special healing abilities.

Soon after, these germs of skepticism began to reproduce. Some considered the movement dangerous, particularly the use of death fantasies, in which guests met in groups to discuss fictional narratives about their own deaths.

In November 2003, Shannon Lewis, a former guest, accused Marshal of "sexual manipulation" during her public turn on the show. Lewis claimed that the unreleased footage of her backstage work contained proof of Marshal's lewd behavior, and over the following weeks, hazy, silent video clips from her session ran on news shows, each one depicting Marshal massaging her face and working her torso. The darkened room created an atmosphere of perversity and Lewis's eyes gleamed feline-like from her reclined chair. The images showed no sign of resistance on her end, but this, she claimed, was due to "sedative teas" Marshal had served her beforehand.

Eventually, the unabridged, uncensored tape leaked and circulated online until it reached the frenzied level of ubiquity that needs culture-wide cathartic release. *Saturday Night Live* parodied the tapes in skits that were among their most discussed segments of the year, with Marshal flexing his biceps for the camera and Lewis salaciously waving her butt in response. Over the following months, three other former guests on the show (Monica Lopate-Gonzales, Jon-Jon Devry, N. Yafini) accused Marshal of similar crimes, and set off an internal legal investigation into the show's policies. Viewership reached an all-time high.

The allegations seemed, at least to the bicoastal press, like pure attention-seeking behavior. These were guests who had made their turns, passed briefly through the limelight, and were trying to claw their way back into it. In response, many of the show's previous guests, famous and non-, female and male, stepped forward to assert their positive experiences in session with Marshal. It helped calm the waters, and the lawsuits were eventually dropped due to lack of evidence, but the damage had been done. No amount of endorsement can ever erase the mark of disgrace.

In the face of divisiveness, I tend to double down on my allegiances. So, around that time, I took my own personal plunge into PM. I'd begun thinking of my interviews as a book-length project and felt that, to really give a fair shot at truly understanding, I needed an internal perspective. So I enrolled in a series of sessions with a local practitioner.

Of course, my motivation wasn't just professional. I'd been swimming in and out of poor health without any kind of solid ground beneath my feet for over a decade, and I needed help that no one, I thought, could give me. The antibiotics had worked marvelously at first, but soon I began to feel the distant prickle of gastritis coming round the bend yet again, and I knew the fundamental cause, whatever that might be, had yet to be addressed.

The failed treatments fortified my cynicism toward allopathic medicine. I began rejecting any advice I received from the dozens of supposed experts I'd visited, and sometimes I did the opposite of whatever technique they suggested. I just couldn't bring myself to believe in their systems anymore, and after seeing the success of Marshal, I could no longer deny the movement's potential.

I received my sessions at the Los Angeles PM center with practitioner Larry Allen Davis, and worked on a standard six-month crawl toward a soft turn. Every morning, I'd perform a whole series of activities Davis assigned to me: gargling with bitter oils, smelling my armpits, splashing icy water on my face, drinking a foul-tasting cocktail of herbal tinctures that made my tongue go numb. In sessions, we'd leaf through my childhood photos, making comments, acting out scenes from my past. The work was alternately enjoyable, tiresome, uncomfortable, and boring.

For me, the most amusing aspect was the audio adaptation. During sessions, Davis played recordings he had made at the address of my childhood home in San Francisco. You could hear the car alarms, church bells, kids screaming. These would bleed into other biographical recordings—from my grade school, high school, the picnic table where I first had my heart viciously broken, my favorite childhood restaurant, etc. I'd also play these at home, or take walks while listening to them on headphones. The intention, as I understood it, was to disarm and demystify my memories.

The most important part of the routine, he said, was storytelling. Davis would recite a different story each week and I'd have to verbally memorize it and speak it aloud to myself three times in the morning. (No writing was allowed. I must truly internalize it.) The stories were all about metamorphosis—a boar changes to cat to plant to rock—and they were set up almost like jokes, with punch lines and rhyming phrases and reveals at the end. (I'd share one here, but the stories are meant to be heard only by my practitioner and me, and are said to lose effectiveness when revealed to others.) Davis asked me to work on my oration so that I could express the meaning of each phrase of the story—adding emphasis on certain words, taking pauses at the right moments—as if I were telling the story to a child in the most generous, lucid way possible.

After all this work, however, the results remained fuzzy. Davis informed me that I was partially "resilient" to turning, a diagnosis that occurs in about 20 percent of candidates, and that I was suited for slower, less dramatic changes in lifestyle. I could continue to do personality work with him, he said, but he wouldn't be able to take me through a full turn, and I could not expect to ever truly forget myself.

This was a disappointment. Despite my years of botched therapies, I still clung to some hope that PM might be the great panacea. I wanted to be assured that I had traveled as far as possible from the sick person of '94, but it seemed that I would not find that kind of assurance with Davis.

I don't want to make it seem like my training was useless. I learned to "draw knowledge" out of my face and shoulders and place it into my feet, which became a pretty useful practice for me at night, when I get caught up in insomnia and circular thinking. I was also able to desensitize certain pressure points in my stomach, and with the help of breath work, I experienced a few, remarkable lungfuls of ignorance.

Most memorably, the treatment taught me to construct my own p chart, something I'd been curious about for a long time, having seen them on the show, but had never fully understood. I'd heard of people having profound revelations on completion of their charts, which, clearly, was an experience I was after. The idea was that a person could view their lifestyle patterns in a visual landscape of peaks and valleys, and somehow the question of their existence would become instantaneously, ineffably answered.

I remember finishing mine while sitting on my patio. I'd been glancing from Mayah's chart-making instruction manual, *Keeping Track of Yourself*, to my scrawled notes, back and forth, making hash marks for my thirtieth year, when I felt my skin tighten, my pulse quicken, and my brain snap into place. I couldn't deny it.

After that, I stared blankly at the sky for a few hours and

indeed, I saw my whole life story, every step of it, suddenly make a kind of sense. Each failure was perfect. My left index toe, essential. Every quality I detested in myself seemed to exist for the sake of some greater balance. It's not the easiest feeling to depict on paper, and yet, the chart had forced me to do exactly that.

And what I came to understand, through Davis's interpretation of it, was how my lifestyle had nurtured my sickness. As he saw it, I jeopardized my health through a series of events. A devastating breakup. An estrangement from childhood friends. A move across the country. The death of my father. My indiscriminate consumption of culture. These, Davis said, weakened me, invasive microbial bodies took over, and pretty soon I began believing in my own illness.

That revelation was perhaps the first moment I felt my nervous system loosen. It's an experience I haven't been able to replicate since, but that night I let myself give in to the abstract, woo-woo feelings I had always kept at a reasonable distance. I became one of the obnoxious many who carried a copy of my chart folded into my pocket, explaining it to any friend too polite to refuse me.

Soon after, I contacted Marshal's office and set up an interview with him for *PMLA*, the Los Angeles PM chapter's newspaper. The editor and I had become friends, and he had casually suggested that I do a talk for them. I'd been waiting for an opportunity to speak with Marshal again, and the whole charting experience gave me confidence that the right moment had arrived.

My intention for this interview was to reinvent my approach, to demonstrate some kind of personal evolution in style from the previous dialogue. Toward Marshal, I would subtly reveal my loyalty to PM—no gushing—and then perhaps, I'd bring up the allegations against his character. I wouldn't prod. I'd simply give him a platform to express his perspective.

To conduct the interview, I flew to New York and stayed with a friend in Brooklyn. Marshal was in New York to speak with prospective guests and to do press, and I'd been meaning to visit anyway. Our talk took place several hours before Marshal's second appearance on *The Late Show*. It was the episode in which he memorably stripped off his shirt to reveal a bright green heart painted on his chest and then smeared chocolate syrup on David Letterman's face. I remember watching it and feeling as if the menacing residue of the trial controversy might have finally dissipated. It hadn't, of course, but that night, Marshal made us all think that it had.

In 2004, we met in the morning at a private apartment in midtown Manhattan. It seemed to be a temporary space, perhaps owned by the network, and was clean and impersonal. The only Isle-related artifacts I saw were a massage table, a kitchen counter lined with medicine jars, and a pair of gravity boots in the corner for hanging upside down, which I knew was one of Marshal's daily practices.

I remember, on that day, how eerily similar he looked to the last time we spoke, as if no single hair or pore had been disturbed. He wore a thick-knit chestnut sweater, and spoke with an increasingly refined articulation, the kind I'd expect of an academic. His assistant fixed us some tea and fruit, and I noticed a glimmer of star worship in her eye. It was a quality I was surprised to see Marshal surround himself with, but one that is probably inevitable in his professional circles. Before she left, she announced to Marshal: "I'll just be in the next room if you need me," as if, at any moment, I might flip unhinged and smother the defenseless man before me.

He laughed off her comment, saying, "I think we'll be OK."

But then, in a masterful twist, he glanced at me, cocked his eyebrow, and added, "Won't we?" as if bringing me into the joke.

This was impeccable social grace. Here was a man under attack by all of culture, and still, here he was, tending to the most minor social blemishes. Even in the face of mass criticism, he refused to close his eyes to the considerations of others.

The following conversation lasted for ninety minutes. As we spoke, two videographers documented us for an upcoming season of *Mayah!*

* * *

MARSHAL ISLE: I just read our interview from 2002. An old issue of the book was in the studio and I was between guests so I opened it up and there we were.

INTERVIEWER: The book?

MI: Oh, that's what we call it around here. *Turnstyle.* It started as a joke, but now it's just what we say.

I: But you don't read, right?

MI: I don't. I didn't read it myself. I asked Gary [Gary Joyce, Marshal's assistant] to do the whole thing aloud. I love the spoken word. And Gary does such great voices. He knows how to do me and he made you sound like quite the distinguished interviewer. But what's funny is, half of what I said isn't true anymore. It might have been true that day, that week, but not now.

I: Did that bother you?

MI: No, it's wonderful. I meant it all. I stood behind whatever p was flowing through me that afternoon. Thank you for capturing whoever that was. *[laughs]* People are so afraid of contradicting themselves, but that ability, to see both sides—that's a personality's greatest gift.

I: Do you still record yourself speaking every day?

MI: Did I tell you that?

I: I read it somewhere.

MI: Yes, I do. First thing every morn. I'm up at 6:52 and I'm talking with the dream still clinging to me.

I: Why 6:52?

MI: It's usually near the end of my sleep cycle, but it's a time I would never wake up if I were left undisturbed. So I always wake a little confused.

I: Which is what you want.

MI: Oh yes. Best time of day. I'm always trying to explain to my guests how wonderful confusion is, but no one seems to have my appetite for it. *[laughs]* Personally, I have to give myself a little confusion every day. Otherwise I start to miss it. Even in the morning, I usually start thinking within a few moments, but if I'm paying attention, I can hold on to it a little longer.

I: Does it work every morning?

MI: Nothing always works.

I: And how would you describe that feeling?

MI: I wouldn't. Doesn't help anyone to describe something like that. Might even ruin it.

I: You tend to avoid descriptions in general, right? Especially when it comes to personality.

MI: To describe a personality is to murder it! No one is really "tenacious" or "compassionate" or "cruel" all the time. To shrink their personality into such words is disrespectful. What we should be talking about are symptoms. The wooden taste in your mouth, how much mucus clings to the rim of your nostril. This is where the personality lives.

I: We talked about some of this before.

MI: Ah, repeating myself again. *[laughs]*

I: No, it's not a problem. Repetition is sacred, right?

MI: That's right.

I: And this morning ritual seems like that kind of sacredness, right?

MI: Yes, and the confusion is also sacred. It pulls me away from the nasty habit of describing myself. That's why I immediately begin talking. Before I do anything. Before I wiggle a baby finger. *[wiggles his little finger at me]* I want all my epithelial tissue to be perfectly still.

I: I don't know if this is related, but I've noticed that I often remember my dreams more vividly if I lie in bed and think about them before moving a muscle.

MI: Yes. Just like that. For me, I wait till I've fully emptied my p into the recorder. Then I move. But barely. I sway a little. I pull my knees to my chest and rock myself, side to side. Warming up. Warming up. And I'm out of bed and creeping.

I: Still talking.

MI: The whole time I'm talking! And I can hear myself filling up a little more with every step. P starts pumping, becoming public. And that's good. I just want to keep the p loose, fluent, so that when Gary comes in, I can give him a shot of semen for the freezer. It should be a very quick thing. I'm usually ready to pop at that point anyway. I barely need to touch myself. The recording's quite exciting. It gets me going. I'm fully erect by the end of it.

I: You do this every day?

MI: When I can. I try to be moderate. I wouldn't want to shorten my lifespan by dumping too much p this way. Usually I'll sip on some wild yam and nettle juice to replenish myself afterward. Maybe I'll eat some pine pollen. But I do try to be thorough about it. If I feel even a mild change in p that day, I make sure to document it. I want to get that configuration of myself down.

I: Why?

MI: Same reason I speak into the recorder. Same reason I have a schedule. Logging the p. If you don't mark it down it gets away from you.

I: You really think it changes every day?

MI: If I made a child today, would it be a different one than the child I make tomorrow? Of course it would. Different day, different offspring.

I: Do you do all this even if someone is staying over in your bed?

MI: I don't allow people to sleep in my bed. It requires too much of me. I need my time in the morning. I know that other people enjoy it, but it's not for me. I realize it comes across as a bit monkish when I say this, but I believe I have a duty as a public figure, and to fulfill that, I need to conserve p and use it judiciously.

I: Do you get irritated by people prying into your life like I'm doing now?

MI: No, but I do think that the less people know about me the more successful I can be at my work. When making turns I need to push people in certain ways, and if they're thinking about my personality, they might be distracted.

I: You say this, but then you date these actresses and models. I mean, clearly people are going to notice this. You could choose anyone, but you choose high-profile individuals, and you go on these late night shows, like you're doing in a few hours, and all that draws attention to you.

MI: But that's good. It creates awareness about the movement.

I: Your romantic life does?

MI: Everyone always wants to know how to make their p more attractive. It's what drives most of the turns we make. If I have that powerful attractive p, they'll be more likely to trust me with their turns.

I: Sounds like it's a tricky balance between nurturing the public life and maintaining the private one.

MI: That balance, if you can achieve it—that's being a true celebrity.

I: How does this balance relate to the recent accusations of sexual harassment? Did those upset the balance?

MI: No, it makes sense. I have to account for that. Because that's what those guests had to do. It was a natural part of their personalities—to accuse me.

I: None of them took a full turn, right?

MI: That's right.

I: So, if you could do it differently, would you want to give them full turns so that you could remove that accusatory aspect of their personality?

MI: Sounds like you're describing a surgical procedure. But we try to avoid that image of *dissecting* personality. I know it's been used before, but I don't like it. And it's also important to remember that turning is not always about getting *better.*

I: "Real Change Can't Be All Good."[5]

MI: Yes. Turning isn't the same as improving. Medicine is both good and bad for you, right?

I: But why change if it's not toward something good?

MI: You're changing whether you like it or not. I just want to help you direct it.

I: But these guests, they didn't seem to understand that. They feel like the experience corrupted them somehow.

MI: I'll say this, everything happened just like they said it did. Some of their ideas about my intentions—I don't agree with those—but that's to be expected. The way I work, I like to

---

[5] The title of Mayah Isle's 2003 book from Hyperion.

be physically involved in the turn. It's intimate. It has to be because it's about intimacy. We're hugging and rolling around together. I cuddle every guest for at least a half hour a day. My hands touch every point on their body at least once. Without that kind of work the guest can only take the turn so far. I truly believe that. The p is in the skin and nerves and muscles, especially the maxillofacial ones *[running hands along his face]* and the pelvic floor. It's a real substance, p. It has a weight. So I have to treat it that way.

I: Talk's not enough.

MI: The point is to stimulate the movement of p. It should be all over the body, and if it's not, if it's inert in certain areas, I want to move it and remind the body that it can flow through there. I can do this with aromatic salves in the armpit or touching inside the cavities. These are vulnerable zones, I know, but indispensable ones. All the guests know this is the procedure. It's not a secret.

I: They knew what was coming.

MI: And during the experience itself these guests were very playful, joyful. You can clearly see that on the tapes. I spend weeks sensitizing myself to every aspect of their mood and body language, and I would confidently say that each of these personalities was comfortable and relaxed and satisfied as they took their turn. Otherwise, it wouldn't have happened. I promise you. We never force it.

I: OK, but specifically, Shannon Lewis—what's your account of what happened with her?

MI: Again, what she says happened is true.

I: But still, I'd like to hear you tell it, if you don't mind.

MI: When Mrs. Lewis started taking her turn—I don't know how much she remembers, but it was a violent process. The whole thing. She was bound to her personality. We'd watched her application tape and spoken to her several times, both at the studio and at her home in Greensboro [North Carolina] where we met her son and a few of her neighbors, and all of it made her seem like an ideal guest for the show. Receptive and excited. Even the optics of it were promising: such a stunningly beautiful woman with such a terrible skin problem.

I: Rosacea, right?

MI: Some people call it that. I don't. But it had spread across her face and lips and eyelids. Certainly the most crippling case Mayah or I had ever seen. By the time we came to her she'd become somewhat of a shut-in. She had highly complicated issues around food, only eating certain macronutrients in certain orders. Carbs before fats before protein. And she wouldn't even hug her son out of a paranoia that her disease was contagious, which, of course, it wasn't. She'd been to all kinds of dermatologists, all of whom were unable to help. And that's when she sent in the application tape.

I: You'd had success in the previous season with a similar case.

MI: Yes. Another man—Mr. Gorre—with severe yellowing of the epidermis. He was told by several physicians that the condition was caused by an allergy, but when he took a soft turn it utterly cured him of it. His new personality didn't have the same allergy.

I: I've read a few documented cases of this type of thing with skin disorders, actually. Even people with multiple personality disorders display different physical symptoms from one personality to another. And you can see it right on their skin. One persona might have an allergy to dogs, while the other has none at all. There are even instances of scars from one personality that start healing once the other personality takes over.

MI: Right, and yet, despite all of this and how receptive Mrs. Lewis initially was, when it came down to the actual turn she was powerfully resistant. She fought against every move we tried. I don't think she remembers much of this, but you can see it on the tape. She wouldn't calm down. I couldn't gently finger-massage it out, which is what I usually do—I had to pop it out with force. And this was when Mayah was off filming the Hawaii special and I was alone, other than hair and makeup and the tub manager. So I had to make that critical decision by myself.

I: And so, how was she being violent?

MI: It started when I was leaning over her, checking her breath with my finger under her nose. I'd put a dab of vetiver oil on my hand to get the p aroused—this is something I do all the time, to everyone—and as soon as she smelled it she sat fully upright and stared straight at me, which is a response I'd never seen before. She was leaning into me, pushing on me. At first I thought she wanted to smell the oil on my finger but then she opened her mouth and bared her teeth and tried to bite me. And when I pulled my hand away, she threw off her robe in protest and stomped around the room. She climbed into her bed and kicked off the pillows and blankets, which is when I knew something had shifted, since up until that point she'd been quite fastidious about keeping her bed made. She knocked over a few bottles of her fluids on her bedside table and crushed the glass with her bare feet and started bleeding. She started making inorganic moves, refused to look me in the eyes—it was bad.

I: She was in some kind of liminal state.

MI: The thing was, she wasn't a problem when she was down, but a guest needs to sit up, move around, keep the blood chugging to all four limbs. You've got to arouse them a little or the muscles can't learn their new moves. Usually, after the first session I'll put a guest upright and walk them around the room, have them try a few things—sit in a chair, use the toilet. Basics. And this is when you can see all the little pockets of new p in them start to open up. That's how it usually goes. But Mrs. Lewis—when I pulled her awake with the oil, she was like a coiled snake, all jammed up with anxiety.

I: Had you ever seen a guest like that before?

MI: Not exactly like that, no. So that's when I helped her across the room and asked her to bend over her tray table, keeping her back straight but her shoulders relaxed, and I placed a small, conical pillow under her sternum, right on the ileocecal valve. It was a position where she couldn't see me, what I was doing, which was important. She was overreactive. Her senses were fuming up. I wanted her to just feel, not to see.

I: How'd you manage to calm her down enough to do that?

MI: I just had to explain it to her.

I: In the tape it's hard to tell what's going on at this point. She relaxes pretty dramatically in a matter of seconds.

MI: I think there's always a way to explain the situation, and in this case, when a person is in that kind of state, it requires a familiar language.

I: Like what?

MI: It would sound silly if I started saying these things here, now. It's more about *how* I speak than what I say. It's very soft and sweet, the way I do it. I'll usually use some family talk, too, to keep myself as friendly as possible. Words you'd only say to family.

I: Like how you'd talk to a baby or a pet?

MI: It's such an attractive sound that people can make.

I: This phrase "pelican little." I've read that's the name her husband called her when they were intimate.

MI: Yes, family talk.

I: Is this the kind of talk you used to calm her down?

MI: Yes, but I only did so with her permission. That's important. She and her husband showed me their private language. They were happy to. They used it in front of me, very openly demonstrating when and how they spoke, what gestures went along with what words. We never trick anyone. I'd like to make that clear. And this is also why the case was eventually dismissed. Even if she felt we somehow deceived her, it isn't true. We record everything and can rewatch all the preliminary meetings and you can hear us directly state all of this to her before she signed the contract.

I: Do you ask this same intimate information from everyone?

MI: For full turns, yes. Mrs. Lewis wanted to take a full turn, and you can't do that without being fully vulnerable. It just won't happen.

I: And "button"—I've heard that word used.

MI: It's already gotten out, yes. This is what her husband called it when he tickled her bottom.

I: Her anus.

MI: Yes.

I: And he had her bend over, like you did, when he did it.

MI: Yes.

I: So can you walk through what you did? This seems to be the moment in question.

MI: Yes. I began by walking my hand up and down her spine until she relaxed. Then I moved to her button, just making the tiniest possible circles on the pinkest, most sensitive part of the skin.

I: This is his technique?

MI: Yes, he taught me.

I: So you had her over the couch and her robe was pulled up and she was what—was she in a kind of trance?

MI: She was very pleased at the time. And I knew she would be. You have to understand that I wasn't inventing this situation. I knew what I would do and she knew what I would do. Her husband told me what to say and showed me his moves and explained how she'd react. This is all documented on tape. I knew everything. How she splayed her fingers in a certain way so that her nipple would fit right between them. How she'd squeeze in quick little pulses. How she shook her hips and sighed.

I: And so what did you say to her?

MI: I said *[in a lilting, cheerful voice]* "Pelican Little. C'mover here and let me push on that button." And she came right to me. That's all I had to say. Exactly how we'd rehearsed it.

I: That voice—is that how he says it?

MI: Yes.

I: Were you sexually aroused at the time?

MI: Yes.

I: Is that normal?

MI: Yes, I felt aroused. If I hadn't, that would have been problematic. And false. And inauthentic. Which is the worst way to bring a personality into this world—though I realize that everyone does not agree with me on this point. Her experience, however, wasn't sexual. She wasn't aware.

I: I just think people expect emotional distance from practitioners of any kind.

MI: I was doing this for *her.* Remember that. It's not exactly what I might enjoy doing myself. It's what *she* liked. And I couldn't be sincerely engaged in this act if I had no arousal. That would've been false. It would have been acting. But that's not what I do. I'm not an actor.

I: Her claim was that, she said she would have never let you do those things to her if she were conscious.

MI: It's true. Once she saw the tape, she wouldn't allow us to show the footage to the audience, which is something we always do. Mayah and I both feel that the more we show people what real experiences with p look like, the more people will understand. Even if it's complicated to watch. But I believe in culture. I believe that people know what to do with this information. But we didn't screen it. She took a copy of the recording for herself and that was it. It was only her later allegations that forced the tape out publicly and spread it around the Internet.

I: And it—the tape, it's missing the sound, which is half of the information, right? When you used her husband's voice a few minutes ago, I realized that I had no sense of what was said in the video, or how it was said.

MI: Yes. And the video doesn't allow you to smell the coriander or hear the deep C sharp frequency vibrating the floorboards through a pair of woofers. And that's all a part of it. But alas, we live in a visual world.

I: Speaking of visuals, I don't know if this is odd for you, or if I'm overstepping some kind of boundary here, but I brought in my chart with me.

MI: Here?

I: Yeah, if that's OK. *[removes papers from bag]*

MI: When did you complete this?

I: After our last talk. I spent a few weeks on it, and I wonder if you'd just take a look with me. Maybe walk me through your reading of it. I thought it might be useful for the interview. To help readers learn how a chart is read.

MI: Sure, sure . . . *[looks at the chart]* So . . . OK, I haven't looked at one of these in a while.

I: You don't read these?

MI: I have. I can. It's just not what I normally do.

I: Oh, well, if—

MI: But let me give this a shot. *[pause]* It'll be fun. I think I see what you've done here. So from this it looks like you started experiencing p at about eleven or twelve years old.

I: Yeah, exactly. That's a pretty average age, right?

MI: And it was public . . .

I: Oh, for sure. I would say that, at that age, that was the first time I could really assert any kind of personality, and I could only do so when other people were around. It wouldn't happen with my parents or when I was alone.

MI: And it looks like it was a slow process for you.

I: Right. And where it happened, over time, was in the classroom, at school. I wasn't really athletic or smart or dumb, or any of these categories that kids start getting fitted into around junior high. I was just blank. I was always that way, I guess. But I'd definitely noticed that other kids had developed, personality-wise, and I remember thinking that I'd probably just always be that way—neutral. And I'd never have the kind of electricity that all these other kids had. But then, in seventh grade or so, I noticed that I was starting to act differently. Almost like I was possessed by a spirit. That's how I thought about it. And I found myself raising my hand to answer the teacher's questions.

MI: Yes.

I: Which was something I'd never really done before. Not that—I wasn't shy, I just wasn't particularly outspoken. And I started answering every question the teacher asked, even if I didn't know what to say. Usually I didn't even have the right answer, and sometimes I wasn't sure what we were discussing. So if we were in, say, history class, I wouldn't even have a sense of what era or what country we were talking about, and if that was the case, I'd just crack a joke. A funny one. And it was great. I just wanted to talk. I had something to get out.

MI: You couldn't control it.

I: I couldn't. And part of what I liked about it was just dropping myself into a situation and seeing what would happen. I started getting in trouble with the teachers and I started studying, and I remember thinking, *Oh, this is me, finally! This is who I am!* It felt like I'd found my role. And I just remember how good and warm it was to soak up everyone's attention. Whereas before I thought of everyone as strangers.

MI: So people reacted well to how you were changing.

I: Oh, yeah, that was the whole thing. I realized that these people around me thought I was amusing. And what's better than that? I think most people would agree that the feeling of someone laughing at a joke that you just invented, in that minute, in your mind, as a reaction to the situation you're in—that's one of the great satisfactions in life, right? You're seeing your environment in a way that has real value to people.

MI: Were these new people you were surrounded by?

I: No, not at all. Same old kids I'd known most of my life, but something changed and I started seeing them differently, like they were my audience. And they started seeing me differently. I'd jump onto my desk and do a little dance or I'd start singing in the middle of class just because I felt some kind of primal urge to do so. And everyone loved it. I knew what to do. I was well liked without even trying to be.

MI: Naturally.

I: And I remember, this is the time when I started getting this feeling like I wasn't the only one looking through my eyes anymore. I imagined everyone in my class could see what I saw, all the time, and I had to act in a certain way all the time. Like, even when I was at home, alone, I wouldn't masturbate or look at myself naked or even pig out on crappy food, because I didn't want them to see me like that. I was performing nonstop.

MI: And you liked that.

I: I loved it.

MI: But looking at the chart, it seems as if this were just temporary.

I: Yeah, it was as if I was on some kind of drug for that period. It lasted about half the school year, but then summer break came and the kids all went off for summer, and when I came back to school in the fall, I didn't feel the same way. The energy had dispersed. The momentum was gone. I'd still think of jokes, but they would seem forced and embarrassing, and I'd end up keeping my mouth shut. Even when the kids would prod me to hop on my desk or make a joke, I couldn't do it.

MI: What do you think changed?

I: Well, I was thinking about this while making the chart and I think it was as if that previous year was this ideal time where I had enough intelligence to be funny but not enough to be self-aware and judge myself.

MI: Is that what intelligence is to you?

I: I think so, yeah.

MI: Hmmm . . . *[traces his finger across the chart]* . . . and then you . . . the next bump I see here was around the age of fourteen . . .

I: And that was a big one. Big. It really shifted for me, in an instant, when I was sitting under this tree at a park a few blocks away from my school, and there were these three girls with me. I can't even remember their names now. Heather, I think, was one of them, and they were from my school, talking about some teacher, who they all felt was lowering their GPA—whatever—and I remember listening to their voices and something about the intersection of their words, the way they were all speaking at the same instant, it acted like a trigger and I started to feel a change in me. We were learning about the asthenosphere at the time—and I remember imagining that process happening inside of me, the drifting tectonic plates.

MI: Was it pleasurable?

I: Sort of. After it happened, I was just brain dead. I could've been drooling. So it was pretty different from the other experience I mentioned before. This was very brief and personal. I was completely disinterested in other people while it was happening. It was purely internal. But yes, I was definitely excited, especially later that night when I could feel it, even when I was going to sleep. I remember thinking that my life would be marked by that moment. I was aware that everything would be categorized as that which came before and after that moment. And it was. It is. I mean, I had spent years going with my family to weekly Mass, which was all about the soul and being filled with the love of God, but I never experienced any of that in church, that faith feeling, and so when these things happened, it didn't even occur to me that it might be a religious experience. Maybe if I were alive a hundred or a thousand years ago I would have immediately seen it in that religious context. I would have joined the clergy. But for me, I didn't know how to frame it. It seemed so separate from the rest of life. I even thought it was maybe a glimpse of a possible mental illness and I was a little ashamed to mention it to anyone, especially my parents, and too embarrassed to mention it to my friends, thinking it would be viewed as self-indulgent, which I think is something I still feel, right now, talking to you.

MI: Discussing yourself.

I: It's hard for me. But I also think this is what led me here. To interviewing. Being inquisitive for a living. And I think this is one of the things I first related to Mayah and the show. It gave some shape to these kinds of experiences. It's all about questions and answers.

MI: On the chart, it looks like the most recent of your changes was when you met your current partner . . .

I: Yeah, it was—but hey, I feel like this is becoming a long detour. We don't have to walk through this whole chart. I know that takes multiple sessions to do a proper reading and—mostly, I wanted to get your feedback on it to see if it looked like I was on the right track.

MI: Yes. I think you are. But as I was saying, charts aren't my specialty. Other practitioners would be able to go much deeper.

I: You've been spot on so far. I can't believe I talked so much. Verbal purging.

MI: That means it's a sensitive chart on your part. And beautifully rendered. Lovely draftsmanship, too.

I: Thanks. I put some time into it.

MI: My only recommendation would be to fill in some of the interstitial areas. You've focused on these significant experiences here *[gestures to four points on the chart]* but consider some of the troughs, the moments of inactivity, the gaps in memory. Those seemingly empty periods are just as important, if not more so.

I: That's good, yeah. Thanks. I appreciate that. I know our time is limited here.

MI: Don't mind that.

I: But, uh, moving on, another thing I wanted to bring up here, before we're out of time, is what's being called "Broken Leg Personality." I hear that phrase everywhere now since the episode last season when you coined it. I'm curious if you think people are using it correctly.

MI: What do you mean?

I: Well, it's a meme now and it's just—it's like what happened to the word *zen*, which traditionally had this ancient philosophical ineffability, but then people started using it to mean just relaxed and serene. Maybe you can just talk a little bit about how you originally meant BLP? Or maybe just talk about that episode?

MI: Sure. Well, Mrs. Crenshaw was the guest on that episode. She had written to us a few months before and had sent along a series of photos of a fractured leg she'd incurred from a car accident. One of them showed the leg a few hours after being broken, when it was puffy and dark pink. Another showed it a few hours after that, black and blue. Another showed the leg in a cast. Then there were some photos of the leg after it had healed. Her letter was mostly concerned with the leg because she was sure it had affected the way p was flowing through her body. She said she hadn't been the same since she broke it. She thought about it when she woke up, when she fell asleep. She dreamed about it. When it hurt she worried about what the pain meant, and when it didn't hurt she was anxious about when pain would return. It started to dictate all her actions. She wouldn't stand unless she had to, in case she might worsen the leg. And later, when it seemed to be healed, she was afraid she might hurt it again.

I: The cycle of paranoia.

MI: Then she started aiming that fear at her husband. She started telling herself that he wasn't sympathetic enough and she resented him for it, for not being as concerned about the leg as she was. She started questioning his involvement in the accident. He'd been driving when their car was sideswiped by a truck, which forced them up onto the curb and into a bus stop. Luckily, he came out of the crash with just a few minor scrapes. She suffered the more severe injury. And she started thinking that he had done this on purpose, that he didn't like the leg and had somehow steered the car into the bus stop at a particular angle to intentionally break it. Or sever it. At the time she wrote the letter, she was considering elective amputation just to please her husband.

I: But I remember, when you brought him on the show, he had

no idea about any of this. She was too embarrassed to discuss it with him.

MI: Yes.

I: But she's OK discussing it with thirty million viewers?

MI: Sometimes it's the only way. *[laughs]*

I: And your opinion is that this woman needed a personality that could handle the injury better than the one she had.

MI: When your body gets hurt, you point to that injury, and the more you point, the more p gets stored there, in that spot. Injuries don't ever go away, even if they superficially heal. It rains and gets cold and you feel them come back. They're there, under the skin, even when the feeling is too subtle to notice. Maybe you're busy doing other things so you don't mind the sensation, but later, when you're at home alone, when your mind starts pointing again, then the pain becomes as big as your experience. If you move in a certain way, you start to feel it. Then you feel it even when you don't move. You plan your day around it. This is a broken leg personality.

I: When pain controls you.

MI: And it does. Too much pain makes it hard to have a personality at all.

I: Tell me about it.

MI: To have a full personality, you have to make friends with pain. More importantly, you have to expect it. You have to know it's coming for you—here, gone, and then . . . hello, it's here again. That's normal.

I: Periods of sickness are healthy, in the scheme of things.

MI: Illness is a part of life. Accommodate it.

I: So with Mrs. Crenshaw, you gave her a kind of pain treatment.

MI: Yes. This is a part of rehab. As soon as we work out all the glows and the moves, we work on pain management. Everyone has their own definition of pain. It's part of what defines their personality. With Mrs. Crenshaw, we focused on the chronic pain in her leg. It was important for her to know that it would always be there. It's real. It would change its shape as time went on, but it would never completely go away. The moments where she didn't feel pain would be special, little fortunes. And to make her feel this way, we gave her pressure lessons and temperature trials.

I: Which have been a bit controversial.

MI: It's nonviolent pain. No one's attacking her. It's inflicted lovingly and with care and in a tranquil setting. No scars. No marks.

I: And the point is to raise her pain threshold, right?

MI: The point is for her to have a good relationship with pain.

I: But isn't pain important? Isn't it basically like an alarm system for the body?

MI: We're not numbing her. We're changing her opinion of it.

I: And how did you know when it worked?

MI: We would ask her how she was doing, and she would say that she was feeling good, even when we knew we had just given her a significant dose of pain, a sensation that she had previously registered as uncomfortable.

I: People say these experiments with pain are irresponsible, especially when you have so many children who idolize you.

MI: I don't think it's very safe for me to accept that responsibility, do you?

I: What about the boy, the teenager in Ohio, who was hospitalized after trying one of these cold-heat trials? From what I understand, he had a grand mal seizure.

MI: He pushed it too far. And so he learned a little bit about the power of pain. But he had no lasting problems from it. Just pure pain. The trials are designed this way, so the pain doesn't hurt the body. It only affects the p. If they follow the practice correctly, if the trial is administered by someone who has absolutely no violence toward you, then I think it would be good for anyone.

I: Even children.

MI: I mean, of course, we suggest different temperatures and pressures at different ages. But I do think children should get involved with their p. Hearing you speak about your own personality development earlier, I wish you had had someone to speak with about what was going on. You'd have a better relationship with your p, which is what we all want, even children.

I: And in terms of self-exploration at that age, it's got to be better than experimenting with synthetic drugs and vandalism.

MI: And what better time to get in touch with pain than the time in life when pain is the most acute—teenagehood. The very age when people start manufacturing their own pain.

I: But the thing is, with these trials, you can't ever know what anyone's intentions are, right? You don't know whether they're doing it for valid reasons. You can put the ideas out there, you can explain it all perfectly, but you can't control how they're used.

MI: Again, it seems you're asking me about taking responsibility.

I: I guess I am.

MI: That's something I can't do. I'm not a guardian. All I can offer are choices.

VII.

April 2006

LOS ANGELES, CA

Before I met the Isles, the path of self-transformation always seemed like a lot of unnecessary huffing and puffing to me. As I saw it, life was a puzzle and I just had to keep going until all the pieces had been rightly put.

For example, in my twenties my plan with food was to dial in my "perfect health" diet. I'd establish some kind of rule set—eliminate nightshades, eat thirty grams of protein thirty minutes after waking, eat fruit on an empty stomach—and then, once all that was locked in, I wouldn't have to consider nutrition for the rest of my life. The anxiety of what to eat for dinner would forever dissipate. Bliss.

And I could do this for everything—wife, work, hair, hygiene, fashion—until I arrived at the flawless life: no more changes. That way, I could focus on the important issues of our time.

But, alas, those were the thoughts of a fool—a "tug," as Masha liked to say. I'd die living like that. Because that's what dead people are: unchanging. The body isn't a permanent thing. It's an eddy in a stream, a temporary accretion of minerals, liquid, and debris.

So I should have expected that the first of my convictions to crumble would be diet. I had, for twenty years, been a vegetarian, identifying with this position on the most fundamental levels—health, morals, ethics. Then, while reading a book on plant intelligence, my confidence withered in a few days. The things plants could do! They're smarter than us. How had I not seen the arrogance of monoculture? We wipe away a vast spectrum of species and replace them with an army of engineered plant clones? This was totalitarianism. How could I ever think plants were more easily sacrificed than animals? And with that, the first pillar of my ideology collapsed.

I had come to PM with a solid history of self-control, but the movement disabused me of that ridiculous impulse. I was no longer a brain riding the horse of my body, drunk on authority. I was the horse. I used to feel pride when people referred to me as a person of principles, as if I were sticking to my ideas in the face of an irrational world, but after PM, I wanted nothing to do with the term. I just wanted to be p.

All this personality crumbling began around the end of Mayah's final season on the show, which I had begun watching, as they say, religiously. At the time, no one knew she was on her way out, of course, but we knew *something* was coming. She loved to drop hints.

On one of the final episodes, she curved her face into a puckish grin, clasped her hands together, and hinted at a "top secret project" she'd been developing behind the scenes.

"I'm so excited to tell you guys what I've been working on," she said.

[massive applause]

"But . . . I can't! Not yet. No matter how much I want to," she said.

[loud booing]

With setups like these, Mayah could milk every drop of anticipation from her audience.

"Believe me, it'll be better if we all wait for it," she said. "For the thrill of it. We don't get many true surprises in life, but I want to give you one of them."

Over the nine months of the show's twentieth season, the blogs and online forums swelled with speculations. Most of these revolved around upcoming celebrity guests, including one persistent rumor about a Supreme Court justice making a turn. Finally, in the premiere of season 21, the show delivered its surprise under the banner of its new, stately name—*M!*

The episode began atypically, with Marshal delivering the opening monologue. He gave updates from the show's twelve-week summer break, demonstrated some seasonal moves ("the autumnal reach"), and described all the new dietary supplements (desiccated beetle carapace, white pine cream) available through the show's website. When the show returned after the first commercial break, the country was introduced to Mull.

I admit, my knee-jerk reaction was not one of open-minded wonder. I wish it had been, but my intellectual prejudices were too deep seated to allow for that. Certainly, a large number of fans now consider the episode a revelation, one of those moments that forever changed their relationship with the world. And I fully believe that Mull deserved this kind of reaction, but all I felt was a knot of fear in my esophagus, which has always been my personal trigger spot.

The media's response was a more dramatic version of my own: conservatives were personally offended by Mayah's choice to dethrone herself from a position of power, and liberals mourned the loss of an icon. One prominent mover called Mull "an affront to the difficulties of mental illness," which got a lot of head-nodding responses from all sides. Several major news outlets claimed, without any evidence, that she was an attempt to cover up a turn gone wrong. These accusations were dismissed, however, when the design plans for Mull were made public and proved how comprehensively premeditated the turn had been.

The response, as divisive as it was, revealed just how emotionally attached the world had become to Mayah. She was at the foundation of contemporary culture and it seemed that she couldn't be removed without devastation. Unfortunately, this made Mull the offender, the one responsible for the loss. She was the big, bad monster of PM before anyone had the chance to know her. The world, it seemed, was not ready.

The polemic surrounding Mull didn't seem to hurt the show's popularity, though, and while she certainly alienated some, she drew in others. Those who had loathed Mayah's new-age pomp seemed to have an immediate connection with Mull's earnestness. A few of Mayah's old friends called her a "cherub" and viewed the transformation as a kind of altruistic sacrifice. For them, her new, plump figure and the smiling, dreamy look in her eyes suggested an undisturbed inner life of good intentions. Her personality was ideally tuned to her body.

Shortly after the season premiere, I remember trawling through the online blog, *Mayahalive.com*, and discovering a whole network of male fans (mostly blogging under mythological avatars) who had arrived to the show only once Marshal had assumed the role of primary host. On another blog, I found a small niche group—Mullies—who regularly discussed their sexual fantasies surrounding Mull.

But the controversy was too much for the network. After Marshal's sexual harassment lawsuits, Mull's questionable personality couldn't be overlooked, and an informal public investigation began. In what was often called the "Isle Trial," the show was probed from every angle and forced to expose its internal workings. NBC ran a clinical documentary, dissecting the precise techniques used for turning, as if they were nothing but a series of mechanistic actions. The FDA began releasing reports on the Isle line of herbs and supplements. The FCC held an internal investigation about Mull's turning process, which was partly leaked by a few gossip magazines. A new reality show, *The Return*, featured talks with previous guests and crew members describing their experiences—some of them were beneficial, certainly, but the show chose to emphasize more controversial moments for dramatic effect.

It seemed culture had collectively agreed that the era of PM should be over. Even among the many of us who stuck with it, the feeling around the movement was no longer potential, but preservation.

Marshal seemed to take this in stride, and in response, he adopted a more radical approach to hosting. He'd refer to himself as "the problem" or "the villain," and he began shows by laughing at himself, making comments like "Stick around if you'd like me to manipulate you." It was a twisted brand of humor that some of the old fans didn't appreciate. Most movers, however, understood. They too had endured the trial alongside the Isles, forced to watch as their leaders' values were cross-examined.

I imagine those who departed from the movement were the same ones who eventually found "the question" (moverspeak for "What is p?") too abstract to handle. Regardless of the hate—or perhaps because of it—the show's ratings continued to rise, and attention aimed toward the show was at an all-time high. Yet it was at this moment, in fall 2005, when Marshal announced that the 2006 season of *M!* would be its last.

Soon after, Isle was approached by National Public Radio to discuss Mull and the investigation surrounding her transformation. He agreed, with the proviso that I would be the interviewer. "For some reason," his assistant told me, "he feels comfortable with you."

Those days, I was spending the majority of my time ghostwriting a book on detox pathways for a pop nutritionist. I had taken the job mostly for money but also out of an appreciation of the nutritionist's work. Years before, during the depths of my crisis, I experienced some mild temporary relief when I implemented her strict diet protocol (mushrooms, algae, ghee, goat colostrum, etc.) and had since considered her one of the top specialists in her field. Over the years, as I had slowly stepped away from my own self-care, I found myself immersed in health and fitness culture, writing about it for magazines and befriending its minor celebrities.

By 2006, I had blithely forgotten the years of my own personal struggle. My illness hadn't reared its hideous symptoms in at least twenty months. I didn't even notice when the last of the symptoms had left me. Once you achieve full wellness, you realize that it feels like nothing. It's not a thing you can point to, health—it's just the absence of pain. It's dumb air. And I immediately took it for granted. And perhaps that's how it should be. When you feel strong, who cares about suffering? Only in the presence of pain do we force ourselves to think about our health. Nobody wants to change unless they have no other choice.

Occasionally, some errant ache would arise and threaten to send me back to my old wallowy, sick self. In those times, I'd dust off that part of my brain and address the problem. Thankfully, I had put together a dependable kit of techniques I could use in defense. And yet, the most effective of these was immersing myself in PM—reading about it, watching, learning more about its philosophy, and even talking with other movers I'd met, exchanging our interpretations. I'd take breaks from it, but whenever my immune system began to fog over, I found the movement itself to be a healing agent. Not its practices or treatments, just knowing it's there in the world. Just thinking about it.

Those of us who had been with it long enough didn't bother concerning ourselves with the hubbub of the trial, or the show's close. We knew its philosophy was more than its public face. We knew what it had done for us, and no one could tell us different.

So, when the NPR interview came about, I felt eager to show Isle my new, healed self. All my new sensitivities. Once the sick miasma was out of the way, the world had become clear. I really could see the p. People's gaits, the way they swung their arms, their neck positions, this had all become a window into their entire approach to life. I'd never noticed it before, but now it was obvious.

During interviews, I began to have the feeling of slipping away from my body, as if my depth perception were pushing me deep into some pleasurable abyss. My questions became like precise carving tools, so sharp that my subjects would sometimes say my "conversational style" made them feel unstable. I didn't care. I knew this was ultimately an important skill and I was sure Isle would recognize it.

We planned to meet at KCRW studios in Santa Monica to record, but on the scheduled day, Marshal called at the last possible minute to cancel. He explained that he wasn't happy with the quality of his voice that morning and that he would like to reschedule, which we did, for the following week.

For the second attempt, he requested that the interview be conducted at his home in Bel Air, which required a recording engineer and an extensive rig of microphones and cables to be dragged into his living room. Below is a slightly edited transcript of that hour-long radio program.

* * *

INTERVIEWER: I'm here today speaking with Marshal Isle, the host of *M!*

MARSHAL ISLE: Last time we saw each other I had the pleasure of reading your chart. You still working on it, mapping it out?

I: Oh, yes. Trying, trying. *[laughs]*

MI: To be completely honest, my voice isn't all here today, so your listeners will have to make some allowances for me.

I: Are you sick?

MI: No, no, I've just been using it incorrectly. Totally my fault.

I: Screaming? Straining it?

MI: Pushing it. I should be gargling with oil three times a day, stimulating my vagus. All that. But I haven't been. I have no excuse.

I: How is Mull?

MI: Oh, quite well.

I: Really? You'd use that word, *well*?

MI: Yeah, sure.

I: Do you think anyone else agrees with you on that?

MI: They should. But yes, many do.

I: Who?

MI: Anyone who calls her Mull. For me, that's someone on Mull's side. They're using her name. And they can see that she's thriving.

I: But nobody really calls her that, right?

MI: You just did.

I: *[laughs]* I guess I did.

MI: There are many of us. We're the ones who spend time with her, give her attention. That's what matters. People who refuse the name aren't allowed near her.

I: Why do you think they refuse?

MI: It's a form of protest, I guess. People like to act stubborn.

I: Sure, but—

MI: I know some people say it's harmful to encourage her. They prefer to act as if she's not real. They think if they don't acknowledge her, if they don't use her name, she'll go away. So what do they do? They use her old name. But I think we can all agree that she's no longer who she once was, right?

I: Right.

MI: And if everyone can agree on that, then there is clearly one name we should avoid using at this point, right? The one personality we know, for sure, she isn't.

I: They just want Mayah back.

MI: But she's gone.

I: But not everyone sees it that way. They think she can go back to how she was.

MI: I wish those people could realize how confusing it is for her to have one name coming from people who love and support her and another from people who want her to disappear. Remember, we call her Mull for her sake, not ours. It's what *she* wants.

I: But this is nothing new, right? There have always been people who disagree with the movement's practice of name changing.

MI: But you can't deny that people identify with sounds and words, hearing these names over and over, following you throughout your life, wherever you go. Bo, Bo, Bo. Lynn, Lynn, Lynn. What is that doing to you? You have to address that sound, "Bo" or "Lynn," as a part of the *whole* personality. I mean, listen, if someone wants to refuse to use the name "Mull," that's reasonable. OK? But what's hurtful is that most of the people who were a part of the show—the staff, guests, fans—when I see them out there denouncing us, like on that spiteful program, [*The Return*], it's a slap in the face to our life's work. My family.

I: Again, people just miss the powerhouse personality. They're in mourning.

MI: But was it only the powerhouse they loved? How many powerhouses are there in the world? That's the kind of personality everyone wants to have. And I get it. I've made quite a few. There's nothing wrong with that, usually. *[laughs]* But this powerhouse chose to be Mull for the rest of her life. Respect that decision.

I: A lot of people don't believe that. They think Mull is a mistake.

MI: Well, I'm just glad Mull doesn't pay attention to any of this.

I: It's almost as if Mayah engineered Mull to be impervious to all the criticism that her personality would inevitably create.

MI: Of course she did. Always one step ahead.

I: And where did that name come from?

MI: Same as all the guests. She named herself. As soon as she took the turn, we asked her for her name, and she told us.

I: Right, and whatever she said, you just stuck with.

MI: Oh yes. The name is essential. It's the first choice. You have to accept whatever erupts from the guest's mouth. And she has to *feel* the agency. She has to feel herself choosing something. It's hers. The first decision. And as soon as she makes it, you can see all the little glows start to light up.

I: What if a guest doesn't know their name?

MI: We wait till they do. We don't force names. It should come easily.

I: What if they just say their old name?

MI: Then they spend a few more days at the spa, taking lessons.

I: Until they give themselves a new name?

MI: Yes.

I: I've heard a lot of things about Mull's turn and her condition and I have no idea what's true. I mean, I don't know if the pictures I've seen are doctored or if the facts are accurate, and so I want to make it clear that I'm in the dark as much as anyone. Because she hasn't given an interview yet.

MI: No, she's not made for that.

I: So, I guess what I'd like for this interview to do is to clear things up. For everyone.

MI: I appreciate you saying that.

I: And one thing I've heard said is that she can no longer read or write.

MI: That's true. But she doesn't want to.

I: That didn't surprise me much. Because you can't read or write either, yeah?

MI: I get lost when I read. Same thing when I write. Halfway through a sentence my eyes get confused. All the words start spreading.

I: Was that part of your personality design?

MI: It's just the way things happened. It was natural.

I: Same with Mull?

MI: Yeah, natural.

I: And I hear her speaking voice is difficult to understand.

MI: Not for me. Maybe for some.

I: In the first episode she didn't speak. Is that because she couldn't?

MI: She could, but it wouldn't have been right for the show.

I: Not a TV voice.

MI: No, no. But she coos and hums very lovingly. She crawls over, nuzzles my armpit, buzzes into it. But it's all in her own frequencies, those animal tones. She's not just communicating verbally. She's humming through every limb and organ. It's full body talk. She speaks directly and loudly with every part of her. She doesn't have to make noises to be understood. You can feel it when you're with her, but it doesn't translate on TV. She's not made for that medium.

I: But can she use actual words?

MI: Yes, yes, but it's not like you and I use words. It's just not her way. She speaks at a different rate than she thinks. The words aren't in the expected order. She'll give you a few phrases, but they won't make a sentence. And usually some of them will be private words only she understands. But you can hear her intelligence behind them, even if you can't understand it.

I: It's a little shocking to learn all this, because Mayah's voice was so instantly recognizable. She was a real orator.

MI: It's true. Mull breathes through her nose when she talks. It doesn't have a depth or resonance like a lecturer. It's quiet. But that's because it's meant for more intimate communing. But as you know I—I don't particularly enjoy speaking this way about her.

I: What way?

MI: Breaking her into parts. Her voice, her words. It's important for us to understand her without this kind of comparison.

I: To Mayah, you mean. The before and after.

MI: But I do think it's important to talk about her. About Mull. That's why I called you. I want to talk about it. I don't want the public to get too fixated on the Mull they've created. The idea of Mull. There's this sense that she's ruined her life. That she's made a mistake. That she didn't know what she was doing. Everyone loves a good tragedy, but that's just not the case here. Mull is satisfied with herself.

I: Is her health all right?

MI: Oh, yeah. She's living the alkaline life.

I: On the Feather River, right?

MI: She was there, at one point, but she's moving around all the time. It's not—I can't say where she is at the moment.

I: Because of paparazzi?

MI: She doesn't love to stay in one place very long. She thinks of herself as bait. So if she dangles herself out there, in one fixed spot for too long, she'll become food.

I: Bait for who?

MI: Cannibals. Man-eaters. That's just what she calls them.

I: And who's that?

MI: Well, it's—I'll do my best to relay her thoughts on them, but I'm not confident I even fully understand. She has deep-rooted beliefs and she stands by them, but it's almost as if she can't really communicate them to the rest of us. Because they're so deep. She doesn't seem to understand why they would need to be explained. And the cannibals are one of these things. They're not people. It's not like cannibalistic tribes in the jungle. I don't think she's even aware of those. She's talking about something else. It's a personality phenomenon. She's got a whole body of knowledge about this. It's not just unspecific conspiracy theories. She's not paranoid. It all adds up to a very careful lifestyle. Every time we arrive somewhere new she has all these rituals she performs as we enter the area. Like, when we enter a town we have to find the points where electricity enters and the power stations and she has to walk around and listen to the sound of the buzz. We always drive around the town, tracing the electric grid, and it's like she knows exactly where to go. Turn left, turn right, right, straight. She's not even looking at power lines. Her eyes are closed. She's just feeling it. I've seen her do it at least five times now and I still can't say why or how she's doing this. But she gets something out of it. I guess this cannibal phenomenon needs electricity and so we always end up staying in these places that are—they're not powerless, but they're—

I: Off the grid.

MI: Right. Sovereign. We move from house to house. We have a good network of people helping us. They believe in Mull.

I: And they also believe in the cannibals?

MI: We talk to them about it, and Mull explains, in her own way. But honestly, I don't think anyone truly understands but Mull. They don't have to. She doesn't need anyone to believe her. It's just—she has a way about her. There's no burden of understanding. She's not afraid of being perceived as crazy or irrational. And we trust her. Whatever she's doing, we know she's doing it for our best interests.

I: But, for those people who don't seem to think she's healthy, I'm sure all this talk would just encourage them.

MI: Probably.

I: And not just psychologically unhealthy, either. I mean, not to be crude, but she's gained some weight, right?

MI: Yes.

I: Quite a bit, it seems. Maybe even a worrisome amount, right? Which is hard for some of her fans, I think, mostly because Mayah was always so proud about maintaining her figure. That was her thing, proving that she could overcome her habits, her genetics, her past. So, I guess what I'm asking is, do you think Mayah would be disappointed in Mull's weight?

MI: Well . . . I don't think that's a helpful question. It's needlessly hypothetical.

I: Would you call her handicapped?

MI: No.

I: Mentally, I mean.

MI: I know what you mean.

I: But can she feed herself? Because I—

MI: Yes, she can. She doesn't always do the best job, I admit, but she can. Usually, though, we have the staff cook and feed her. She's generally monitored during meals.

I: Monitored?

MI: Well, she likes . . . unusual snacks.

I: I've heard about this—it's called pica, right?—where she eats nonfood items, a lot of metal and wood. Dogs do this. Kids, sometimes.

MI: Roughage, we call it. *[laughs]*

I: Like what?

MI: Anything. Bark, a screw, a coin. She's into the high mineral content. Last week she got into some furry fruit, with all this grey, sparkling mold on it. Someone at the house must've left it in a drawer, and she just went to town on it.

I: She didn't know it was rotten?

MI: Didn't care. And it wasn't a problem. She was fine after it. And she loves to swallow the pebbles from the driveway. *[laughs]* I keep finding her pockets filled with them and I'll see her shaking them around in her hands, popping a few in her mouth.

I: Is she sneaky about it?

MI: She just laughs when I ask her about it. It's—tsch—it's fun for her. She can feel them moving through her body in a way that you can't feel food, which breaks down into mush. She comes up to me and puts my hand on her abdomen where she can feel the pebble passing. It's like she's getting to know herself from the inside out. And she's pretty careful about which stones she picks. She's not just scooping handfuls into her mouth. She's out there in the field, looking for the right ones.

I: And what about dressing herself and just all-around living—

MI: She's fine. But, again, it's hard for her. She doesn't want to think about that quotidian stuff. Eating, dressing. She just wants to be living fully in touch with the p at all times.

I: So she's not self-sufficient.

MI: But remember she chose this. She spent years saving up money for exactly this purpose. To be Mull. She worked toward *this*. And now she's arrived at her masterwork.

I: Really, you'd call Mull that?

MI: Oh, yes. I believe Mull can benefit humanity as a whole if people pay the right kind of attention to her.

I: What's the right kind?

MI: Respect.

I: As opposed to?

MI: Voyeurism. Judgment.

I: Speaking of which, the poster campaign is everywhere . . .[6]

MI: "Free Marshal," right?

I: Yeah. I, actually—I saw a few of them on the way over here. And then there was a sticker of your face on a stop sign. What do you think of all that?

MI: I'm not sure I understand it. I'm trying to fast a bit from media these days, so I haven't been following. The idea is that I'm trapped?

I: Yeah, that the public trial has imprisoned you.

MI: And who is doing this to me?

I: The law, the media, the people.

---

[6] In early 2006, a group of movers created the "Free Marshal" logo as a response to the public witch hunt of PM. It has since appeared on all variety of clothing, building, and printed matter.

MI: Are you doing this to me?

I: *[laughs]* Yeah. That's the idea. Me among others.

MI: Well, I just don't feel that way. Why do people say this?

I: Well, this kind of media-frenzied state is where your personality thrives, but I guess it's just a common sentiment you hear from people under scrutiny. They feel invaded. Claustrophobic. And people just assume you feel that way, too. Especially now, when there's been so much negative attention. Even though, the truth is, people still envy your situation, even if they would likely have a nervous breakdown dealing with the pressure you're dealing with. Even then, they'd still probably choose it, just to be famous.

MI: I appreciate all the sympathy, but honestly, I don't feel imprisoned. I'm not upset. I just wish people would use all this p for their own turns.

I: But the good thing is, in general, you have so many people on your side. That's what this campaign is about. I mean, I drove down Alameda Avenue [where the *Mayah!* studio is located] recently and I couldn't believe it. People were camped out on the sidewalk, right next to the gutter, for days, just to get a seat on the next episode.

MI: Well, those days are no more.

I: Is the show truly over?

MI: Yes. I'll finish out this season on my own, and that'll be the end of our run with NBC.

I: Now, I've heard all kinds of conflicting stories about what's been happening with the end of the show. Do you want to clear anything up here?

MI: It was mutual. With all the controversy, I felt I could no longer operate in a meaningful way with culture. People aren't looking to *M!* for help anymore. They're looking for controversy. It's like you've been saying, the fans have become more . . . fanatical.

I: Have you thought about going back to television after? Because I get the sense, despite all of the complications, that people don't want you to go away. Mayah was what? Fifty-eight? And she'd stopped appearing at the seminars and it seemed to most people—me included—that she was backing away from public life. Right? Long before Mull. And it seemed like you were getting the nod from her to take over. Right? So then, with all that in mind, your willingness to let go of the show at such a young age, that surprises people. You have everyone's attention in the palm of your hand.

MI: Mm. Well, the show needs to end eventually, and I'm just trying to find the right ending.

I: Are you tired of being so public?

MI: No, I'm not tired, but I have to respect my reputation, and it's become clear that it isn't doing too well. It needs rest.

I: Would it be a problem to discuss the investigation for a minute?

MI: Not at all.

I: And you don't have to answer anything you don't want to. I'm not going to try and, and—

MI: I know. I trust you.

I: So I read over the transcripts a few times, but if you're up for it, I'd like to just walk through the evening again.

MI: Sure.

I: Good, and so, to start maybe you could talk about where you were the night of Mull's turn—what you were doing before everything happened.

MI: Where do you want me to begin?

I: How about the studio?

MI: OK, so, around sunset is when we do our checkups with the new guests, and I was in building two, checking in on Mrs. [Rita] Dugard, who was in the spa with a three-hour green mask.

I: Dugard was the guest you were working on at the time.

MI: Yes, but she wasn't mine. She was Mayah's guest and I came to look in on her just for a second opinion. Mayah liked to get my take on certain guests. And Mrs. Dugard seemed like she was rounding the bend on her turn. She was still down and she wasn't getting any jerks, which was good, so I went to Michael's[7] office to get his thoughts about her progress. And he felt she was doing well. It was day eight for her and she seemed to be learning all the moves easily. The plan was for her to be on the show in two days, which seemed feasible.

I: And where was Mayah during all this?

---

[7] Michael Billings served as behaviorist of Peggy Creek Hot Springs from 1998 to 2006.

MI: When I left her, in her dressing room.

I: When was that?

MI: Maybe forty-five minutes beforehand. I was giving her some time alone.

I: Where did you go after the spa?

MI: Backstage. My dressing room. To record what I'd just talked about with Michael.

I: Which you do a lot, because of your memory?

MI: Yes. It's a smidge unreliable. *[laughs]* So that recorder has become an extension of me. My second brain.

I: What did you say into the recorder?

MI: I mentioned Mrs. Dugard's face, which seemed to be responding well to the bentonite-chlorella mask we were using. I said we should expect her to wake up at the right time and that I was pleased about the results. I also recorded what I had eaten that day, which, despite my memory, I can remember pretty well: coconut, avocado, steamed dandelion greens, astragalus broth, duck eggs, beet kvass, a few shakes of cinnamon on wild honey. I've had to listen to the tape so many times, I know it by heart. And I usually mention any moves I'd learned, but that day, I hadn't learned any, so I said that. And then, while I was near the end of my recording, I heard the sounds next door.

I: Thumps, you called them.

MI: Three, yes. Like this. *[pounds fist against table]* And they were followed by a hissing. *[blows air through teeth]*

I: This is coming from the bathroom on the other side of your wall?

MI: Yes. At the time I thought it was the plumbing.

I: So you kept recording.

MI: Yes. I was lying in my hammock, eyes closed, trying to focus.

I: And on the tape you can supposedly hear the thumps and the hissing.

MI: A little. The hissing went on for a long time, even after I stopped recording.

I: What did you do then?

MI: I packed up for the night. I drank my mucilaginous tea. I shut off the lights and went to meet Mayah to leave, which we always did together. And I remember walking down the hall between our rooms and noticing a thick, minty smell. Like camphor. And when I entered her dressing room it became about twice as strong, potent enough to make me get a little dizzy.

I: When Mr. Billings was questioned about the smell, he said he didn't notice it.

MI: Well, I guess he wasn't paying attention.

I: People suggest you invented it.

MI: I'm hypersensitive. It's my job.

I: OK. So you enter the dressing room . . . It's empty, right? Mayah wasn't—

MI: She wasn't at her vanity, where I'd left her earlier, and so I looked for Carla [Moore, Mayah's chief of staff from 2000–2006] but she'd already left.

I: So as far as you knew it was just you in there?

MI: In that studio, yes. Like I said, the manager was in his office behind the soundstage. Everyone else had left for the day.

I: Did you look for Mayah?

MI: I waited for her in her dressing room, expecting her to return in a few minutes, but of course that didn't happen.

I: When did you start to get worried?

MI: I didn't. Mayah's digestive system had been overactive in the last few weeks, so I assumed she was working on a bowel movement. She could spend an hour or so trying to fully eliminate. There was a massage table in there and she'd often lie down, massage her stomach to get the organs moving. It was a whole process.

I: And how long did you wait for Mayah in her dressing room?

MI: I'm told it was twenty minutes or so, but I'm pretty terrible with time.

I: What did you do?

MI: This is when I noticed the henbane. The jar had been sitting on Mayah's dresser for the last few weeks. It was sent to her by one of her herbalists at the Tully Center. We had talked about trying it a few times in the spa, but we hadn't had the chance to do it.

I: When you say "trying it" . . .

MI: It's used topically, mostly, but also ingested in small amounts, the idea being that it simultaneously works from the inside out and outside in. So you use just enough to faintly smell it. That's what the herbalist had recommended. A droplet the size of a grain of rice on a toothpick. But that day, when I saw the jar on her counter, the lid was unscrewed and about half of it had been spooned out.

I: It was what, a thirty-two-ounce jar? That would be enough for a hundred people.

MI: At least.

I: And what were you and Mayah planning to do with it?

MI: It was intended for the "Rebirth" episode. Alan[8] and some of the other producers were concerned that the show had become a little too repetitive, with the same segments and same format, so we'd been considering new exciting directions. The henbane was one of them.

I: You would use it on the guests.

MI: Yes, but we fully intended to experiment on ourselves first. As we always do.

---

[8] Alan Wheeler, the show's executive producer.

I: But initially the herbalist brewed it for Mayah alone. That's what he said.

MI: Yes, to help with some of the heat from her personality. She'd been feeling warm all the time, especially her extremities. Soaking her feet in buckets of ice water. Air conditioning blasting. She couldn't sleep.

I: Menopause.

MI: I wouldn't use that word.

I: And the henbane oil was a sort of a cooling agent?

MI: In a way. I'll show you. Can I borrow your hand for a moment?

I: Sure. *[extends hand]*

MI: *[rubs hand vigorously around I's forearm for a few seconds]* You feel that heat?

I: Yes, from the friction.

MI: But I'm not talking about the *actual* friction. Just the feeling of it. Try to ignore my movement. Focus on the heat coming from the inside . . . The oil was for cooling that kind of heat. And we thought it could be right for making turns because guests often described a similar inner warmth.

I: And so when you saw the jar, what did you think had happened?

MI: I thought Mayah had used it.

I: So then you used a little, too.

MI: Yes.

I: Why?

MI: I wanted to experience it with her.

I: And how did you apply it?

MI: I took off my sandals and rubbed it on the soles of my feet, between the toes and the sensitive parts where the skin isn't as thick. I expected it to be smooth, but the paste was mixed with ground-up bones so it makes tiny cuts to let oil into the bloodstream.

I: Did you know it was blended with amniotic fluid?

MI: Yes, I knew.

I: Did you know it had been illegally obtained?

MI: No, I didn't, and I'm not sure Mayah knew that either.

I: But you were aware it wasn't something you could buy in a standard apothecary.

MI: Sure.

I: Did you feel the effects immediately?

MI: No. I put my sandals back on and wiped my hands with a

towel. As I was doing this I noticed some oil stains on my vest and hat, so I went into the bathroom to clean up, and that's when I found her.

I: Weren't you concerned you'd walk in on her using the toilet—

MI: No. We were always comfortable with each other.

I: And when you discovered her, she was naked, yes?

MI: Yes. She was lying across the countertop with her back toward me, her face toward the mirror, and her eyes open.

I: Did you see the henbane on her?

MI: Oh yeah. Glistening. She'd applied it pretty liberally to her face, eyes, lips, palms, anus, vagina, armpits. All that.

I: Could she speak at this point?

MI: Just that whistling sound I mentioned.

I: The hissing.

MI: Yes. She—I think she had swallowed several tablespoons of oil, which loosened her vocal cords.

I: So no words.

MI: No.

I: And she'd already vomited at this point?

MI: I noticed some of the oil pooling in her mouth and I tipped her head forward to drain it so she wouldn't choke. I don't think she'd put any food into her stomach that day, so there wasn't much.

I: Right. She'd been fasting.

MI: She hadn't been eating lunch with the crew for the last few days and I asked her why and she claimed she was trying to starve the fatigue out of her.

I: But really, she was planning to use the henbane.

MI: Yes.

I: Now, here's the point where a lot of people—they don't understand why you didn't go for help, call the police.

MI: Who could help? I knew what she wanted me to do, and it wasn't rolling her into an ambulance. She and I spoke about this often. She wanted me to keep the p moving, so it didn't get clogged. And so that's what I did. I took her pulse, looked at her tongue, and started rubbing.

I: Now, with Mull this was a radically different sort of turn than she'd done before, right?

MI: Yes.

I: Can you say a little more about that, exactly how Mull was different than what had been done on the show in the past.

MI: When I give lectures, I find it's helpful to use the image of a circle. Have you heard me do this?

I: Yes, but please . . .

MI: So I ask everyone to imagine a circle, on the ground. Close your eyes.

[I closes eyes]

See it cutting a brilliant white line in black space . . . Can you see it?

I: Yes.

MI: But *really* see it. Don't just *think* you see it. And then once you have it there, fixed, move toward it, walking in a straight line until you arrive at its edge. Are you there?

I: Yes.

MI: Now step onto the line.

I: But you're just imagining this—not actually walking?

MI: Yes.

I: OK.

MI: You are now facing its center. So you must turn your body and walk along its edge.

I: Mm hm.

MI: But don't do it yet. Wait. Get ready, in your mind and right before turning . . . stop! Now, notice your muscles. Are some of them already tightened and ready to turn? Are they anticipating it? Even an imaginary turn, even before you've begun to take it, your body often begins to respond.

I: Right, right. I think I feel that.

MI: From now on, as you walk along the circle, you will be in a constant state of turning. You'll begin the turn at zero degrees, and you will walk a quarter of the way around the circle until you reach ninety degrees. Here p is not lost or gained. You can see the point where you began walking and you can also see the corresponding point on the other end of the circle.

I: A soft turn.

MI: The first decade of the show was all about those turns and they were quite successful. A lot of those were made well and were helpful to the guests. But eventually, Mayah found that these would slip. Nothing had been truly forgotten. So regressing was easy. It still felt comfortable. Like a person was returning to their quote true self. We didn't want that, and so Mayah and I began making full turns about seven years ago. These required stepping halfway around the circle. One hundred and eighty degrees.

I: This is when you first came on the show. You were the first full.

MI: Right. We still used the soft turns—but the more we made full turns, the more we knew that we had a responsibility to continue making them.

I: Responsibility?

MI: Yeah, to the world. When a full turn is made well, it's like an orgasm for anyone who ever comes in contact with that person.

I: Whoa.

MI: You've felt it. I know you have.

I: *[laughs]* I have, I have. *[both laugh]* And, at that time, when you came on the scene, there wasn't anyone else doing them, right? Mayah was sort of a pioneer.

MI: Oh yes.

I: But then did Mayah start to feel like the full turns, the one-eighties—they weren't enough? Is that what Mull is about?

MI: Well, well, let me finish here. The full turns were lovely. We weren't stepping away from the full, but even then, we had been talking about going *past* full. We hadn't made any of these yet, but we'd discussed what it meant to go past full. That's all. Just talks. We had no plans or methods on how to accomplish this, but we both knew the step needed to be taken.

I: And *that's* what Mull is.

MI: Yes, she's the first.

I: How would you describe that kind of turn?

MI: The place beyond personality. Where any silly ideas we have about personality break down. As much as we try not to, we still think about personality as a series of parts and traits and behaviors. If someone asks you to describe them, you would begin by choosing their most glaring characteristics and working your way down to the gentler, less conspicuous parts of them, right? And even when we were making the full turns, even when we were trying to think holistically about the personality, we were still essentially addressing them as long lists of information. I realize this now. But we wanted to start seeing it more like a balance.

I: You can't remove someone's sense of humor without also removing their depressive tendencies.

MI: You can't change people specifically. It's a whole ecosystem—take out one part and the whole system falls apart. We wanted to lose control of p and go beyond our conception of personality. And that's what Mull is. She's a patch of wilderness. That personality is just growing and she's being pulled along with it. All day long.

I: What comes after Mull?

MI: The whole exchange. You receive your personality, learn it, work on it, and then pass it along to the next guest. That would be true sustainability. P recycling forever. Every season a new personality. Every moment would be like pure discovery. The first time you eat an apple, over and over again, like seeing the world for the first time forever. No one would have to feel miserable again.

I: But that's only theoretical at this point?

MI: It's an idea. Mull makes it real. Mull was just an idea until she wasn't.

I: But why do you think Mayah made her turn without you?

MI: She didn't.

I: But, I mean, you weren't there when she did it.

MI: Yes I was.

I: But that day, you didn't know it was happening.

MI: She wanted me free from any association. She knew the process wouldn't be accepted by the network, her fans, anyone.

I: But earlier, you were saying you wanted to keep Mayah relaxed, right? And you didn't go for help, and by doing that—or not doing it—you were basically assisting, right? Implicating yourself.

MI: Yes. All she requested was that I keep her nice and open. Parasympathetic. How could I deny her that? So I quieted the p in my voice. I placed her head in my lap, rubbed her facial triggers, and helped her work through every glow.

I: Her face was shaking, you've said.

MI: She was working through her old personality.

I: By this time did you feel the henbane kicking in?

MI: Yes.

I: In the transcript you describe it as a feeling of compassion.

MI: I couldn't feel the hard surfaces around me. The ground, the counter, Mayah's face, which I was touching. It was all just like thick air. And as soon as I felt it, that's when I first saw Mull.

I: What do you mean?

MI: I saw her taking the turn.

I: But she was unconscious?

MI: No, not really. She was starting to glow. I could see it.

I: It's been suggested that the oil you used was basically a placebo, that henbane itself doesn't really do much, that it wasn't particularly active. What do you think of this?

MI: The henbane isn't important. That's true. To me a placebo would be the best possible result. It means that I produced all these feelings, independent of all this material nonsense. *[waves his hand around]*

I: P for placebo.

MI: Yes. *[laughs]*

I: So, as you were relaxing her, did you feel you were just following her plan? The rubbing—this is what she had told you to do?

MI: Yeah, just a basic rub out. Neck, shoulders, colon, fingers, soles, roof of the mouth, backs of knees. Pushing the blood toward the heart, away from the brain. Using three fingers on the delicates.

I: And it helped?

MI: Of course. But again, the rubbing isn't what's important. It's just a way for her to know I'm paying my full attention to her. Only to her. She has to know that and hear my voice and feel my fingers and *feel* that attention. So I begin by doing a *[in a low, soft voice]* "Whhhaaaat?" Like that. "Whhhaaaaaaat?" With my voice going up at the end of the word.

I: The opening call.

MI: It's comforting for her. I'm helping her say goodbye to that personality. And as I do this, I slowly pulled my hands away from her, so that she couldn't perceive the difference. The idea was, if I did it well—and I think I did—her muscles would go limp. No p left. And this is when I began asking *[in gentle voice]* "Where's Mayah?" Just like that. As if I couldn't see her. As if I had nothing in me but plain curiosity. I said, "If only I could find Mayah!! I don't see her anywhere!" But I'm looking right at her the entire time *[staring ahead]* so she knows I *can* see her.

I: Peek-a-boo.

MI: And then I walk around the room and hold any object I find around me, patting down everything like a blind woman. I pick up a lamp *[cradles imaginary lamp]*, a food wrapper *[looks inquisitively at imaginary wrapper]*, and I examine each one. I look through the whole room like this. "Is this Mayah?" I say. "Is this?"

I: And she's lying there watching?

MI: Yes, yes! I step right over her body, as if to me she is no different from the carpeted floor. I inspect a peeling corner of wallpaper, her long wood pipe on the credenza. I ignore her, perfectly, and then, after I've considered everything, I take her arm like this *[lifts limp right arm with left hand]* and look at it very carefully. I inspect her. I touch her legs and I pull on the leg hairs, as if she's just another object.

I: Did she react at all?

MI: Oh no.

I: But weren't you concerned that she was dying?

MI: She was, yes.

I: But it didn't worry you.

MI: No.

I: And so how long did this go on for, with you massaging and playing this game with her?

MI: I felt as if it didn't last long enough. An hour is what I've been told, but I can't say for sure. Henbane undoes the feeling of time. But then Michael interrupted us . . .

I: And called the paramedics.

MI: He insisted that we call, even when I tried to explain the situation to him.

I: I read his testimony and he said when he walked in you were cutting Mayah's hair. Is that right? And that her face was smeared with blood.

MI: Yes, but that blood was already there. I didn't do that. She had done that before I came into the room.

I: She'd cut herself on her forearm, right? With shears.

MI: Yes, to apply the henbane to the wound. But listen, this was a forceful turn. An exploration. She wanted Mull done in a single fluid motion—not labored over for weeks and months. Effortless. We've done years of strenuous, demanding turns, and those are often necessary. People like to feel the strain of a transition. It's important for them to *feel* the work to understand the importance of what they're doing. That's how America is. But Mull was a chance to take a turn without the plaque that can build up over time. Sometimes a moment of violence can communicate with the body in ways that hours of thoughtful work can't.

I: And Mayah was stubborn.

MI: She was a well-developed tree. Like any sprout, it begins thin. You can snap it with fingers. Then it becomes thicker, harder, and you need a pair of scissors to cut it. Later, you need a saw. Then a chainsaw, a machine many times stronger than any human. Mayah was like that.

I: Was Mayah stronger than other personalities?

MI: Oh yes. She strengthened it every day, which is not something most people do. And even if they do, or try to, they certainly haven't been doing it as long as she has.

I: Since she was a kid, right? I remember her describing some of the games she played in the shower—

MI: And nobody—I never saw anybody who was as dedicated to p as she was. It was all she ever thought about.

I: All that being said, do you understand Mull? I mean, why Mayah made that choice?

MI: She always thought her body was aging too quickly for her p. And she was right. It was breaking down. It wasn't meant to be old. These last few years, it was eating away at her.

I: Now that you mention it, Mull doesn't really seem to have an age. Kind of timeless.

MI: As far as she's concerned, she's immortal.

I: I've heard it said that Mull has the personality of a dog.

MI: Yes. I've heard that. It's kind of true. She's not putting so much energy into her personality all the time like the rest of us. She saves it, stores it, and you can feel it. Just to be around her feels healing. The way it feels to be near a good dog. Good warm presence. She doesn't even need to do anything. She's just Mull. The best.

I: Sounds like a comforting presence.

MI: I promise you, nothing is more comforting than Mull.

VIII.

May 2014

LAS VEGAS, NV

In 2013, singer and "chameleon of pop" Maggie began a three-year residency at Caesar's Palace in Las Vegas, Nevada. The series of two hundred highly anticipated concerts at The Colosseum (the Palace's four thousand–seat venue) announced her return from an eight-year hiatus as a performer. The full run of shows sold out in eighteen hours.

The residency received ebullient reviews, even from the writers who had once dismissed Maggie's early hits as populist dreck. It seemed that nostalgia was swinging in her favor, and that her age, stamina, and temporary absence had served her well.

The run at the Palace also marked the beginning of Maggie's collaboration with Marshal, her "personality director," who was himself stepping out after several years away from public life. Many people suspected he was patiently waiting out the ripples of controversy from the so-called Isle Trial, but in fact, he had been spending his time working, quietly, diligently, on himself.

The pairing of the two '90s icons didn't surprise anyone: Maggie (born Margaret Caitlyn Willani) had been a vocal advocate of PM since her second album and even cowrote the international bestselling memoir of her life in the movement, *Singing Without*

P (2008). She has made six turns, all of them publicly—Margaret, Miss Maggie, Mae, Maggie Mala, Magdalena (or Lena), and Maggie. The last of these names both began her career and was now revivifying it twenty-four years later in Vegas. She had come full circle.

Her personality changes were frequent, unabashed, and provocative, especially during the years when she was perceived as a role model for young girls. Her detractors remarked that her turns were cheap stunts. (Michael Jennies at *The Washington Post* famously said her career wouldn't last beyond "the generation of teeny boppers who first adored her.") For her fans, though, Maggie's bouquet of selves was a resounding call for personal growth.

After years of rigorous touring and constant public presence, however, she looked withered—the Lena years—and she decided to step away from attention. The media, for their part, waited to hear the archetypal story: she'd swallowed the wrong cocktail of pills, curled up in her bathtub, and passed on. But instead, years later, all of us were reintroduced to the new Maggie in all her radiating energy—loud and rude with a vocal drawl and a short-short haircut. Somewhere, she had found a fresh source of p, and it seemed she had absorbed it well.

Undoubtedly, her greatest contribution to the movement has been an ability to assess and adapt to her cultural environment. She understands the expectations placed upon her by fans and critics, and she pivots constantly to confront them. As she aged, she recognized what was needed to support her development, reinventing her attitude, style, music, and dance routines to suit her moment in life. The twenty-one-year-old pop star is not a sustainable personality for anyone.

In the last few years, Marshal's presence beside her had seemed to cast a more tasteful light on both of their careers. During the residency, most of his work was done backstage, but occasionally Marshal warmed up the crowd with a soliloquy on his favorite topics. At the concert I attended, he stood onstage in a heather-grey kilt and riffed on cosmetology. He told an anecdote of his recent haircut debacle and how it nearly swept away his personality. "Am I getting weaker, or are the scissors getting sharper?" he said, and they all laughed. He asked any hair stylists in the audience to stand and then clasped his hands together in prayer and bowed to them.

Sometimes Marshal would join Maggie onstage for the encore, when they would engage in some droll, scripted banter before the band stepped into the first tinkling notes of "Name Me," her nightly closer. His primary duties, however, remained hidden, and he offered few public statements about the work. Except for the inclusion of "Marshal Isle Presents" on every Maggie-related billboard in Vegas, he seemed to have stopped pushing himself as a product.

Since the end of *M!*, Marshal's life choices had consistently flummoxed the media. First, his bold refusal of fame. Then, after years of silence, a modest resurrection, not as a star, but as what—a producer? Nobody had the pleasure of announcing "Marshal is back," because he wasn't, not really, not audaciously, not bigger, not hotter. If anything, his presence had become less commanding and more commonplace. Where's the story in that?

From another angle, however, the narrative was clear. When *M!* came to a close, Marshal could see that culture wanted a new kind of personality. Mayah, too, had seen it coming and made her exit accordingly, before her time was up. Magazines didn't want the old A-listers, and fans didn't want magazines. The rise of social media had unleashed a new kind of up-to-the-minute celebrity, able to narrate their own stories in real time. Comparatively, a daily talk show was irrelevant, and a week-long self-transformation was a punishing lesson in patience.

Marshal knew his own personality well enough to understand it could not provide the world with what it needed. Sure, he could've changed to accommodate it, but as I see it (though I don't think he'd ever truly admit this) he didn't want to forget about Marshal. He'd grown attached to it, and he knew, even if he did give it up, that no one could possibly guide him to a better self. This man had defined the contemporary turn, and the only person who could improve upon it—Mayah—was gone. Or maybe some splinter of Masha still remained inside him, afraid to return to the hotplate of celebrity, and it just wanted to be left alone.

This may sound like blasphemy to some readers—and perhaps I'm way off in my assessments—but part of my intention in publishing these talks is to allow a little uncertainty into the discussion. I think Mayah wanted this, too, and I only fully decided to publish the talks when she called me, years before Mull entered the world, and finally gave me permission to publish.

"Eventually," she said, "when the time feels right, show the world the boy we raised. Warts and all. They won't get it. It'll destroy my reputation. But that's fine. If all goes well, I hope my reputation is destroyed by then anyway. It's the only way I can move on."

I don't have any interest in staining Marshal's reputation. I want to see him as a full human being. He wasn't a saint and he had no interest in becoming one. A saint lives perfectly within a system of standards. She abstains, performs, eats, and breathes inside that system. She creates a single, clean self and never strays from it. But the problem is, when those standards are no longer important to culture, her sainthood is obsolete. If the world no longer values the virtue of modesty, a humble saint holds no value.

But Marshal escaped his sainthood. He recognized the velvet prison of PM, of culture, and planned his getaway. He did this not by simply leaping from one prison to another, but by transitioning to a way of living that was beyond imprisonment.

After my conversation with Isle in 2006, I took many trips to Las Vegas to visit him. I despise the town, but when he mentioned in an email that I should stop by to see him, I told him that I had plans to pass through later that month—a fib—and soon found myself in his hotel room, drinking a cocktail of prickly pear juice and absinthe.

It took me no more than a few minutes to notice that Isle's personality had become something altogether different from the one I had last interviewed. I asked him if he had made a turn, and he responded that he "didn't have to," as if he were done with the whole enterprise of the personality arts.

As we continued to speak, I noticed that Isle had picked up a habit of wiggling his fingers and spreading the toes of his bare feet. It was subtle, at first, almost like a tremor, but the more absinthe he drank, the more apparent the movement became, until it looked as if he was tapping along to a rhythm only he could hear. I assumed it was some kind of fasciculation, like the ones I sometimes experienced, but when I finally asked him about it, he told me he was "remembering how to act around [me]."

These tics, he said, allowed him to access a memory bank of behaviors he'd been rehearsing for up to ten hours every day. Furthermore, what he called "remembering" wasn't *recalling* an event, but *becoming* a new personality. Constantly. In other words, he was attempting to embody a new fully developed attitude, worldview, and physicality in every breath.

What I began to learn over the next few hours was that Marshal had spent much of the last decade developing personalities for every situation—hundreds of them, an entire internal society of his own making. During his time on the show, he was accumulating these personalities, describing them in charts, drawing out their movements. But rather than cataloging them by name, he programmed them into his memory with combinations of slight, almost imperceptible movements. As he saw it, the personalities *were* the movements, and through these wiggles, these triggers, he was able to dance through a cascade of selves, perpetually changing, never settling on a single one for more than a few moments. By moving in these ways, he was constantly refreshing himself, existing in perfect transcendent concentration.

We spent that first night discussing this philosophy. As he saw it, the process related to what neurologists called "mirror neurons," the cells that allow us to mimic the world around us.

"I just want to be like water," he said, once. "No form. No conflict."

In the morning, he asked if I would continue to visit him and continue the conversation. I had been the first person with whom he'd shared these ideas, and he hoped that he could work on them with me openly so that I could help him address the flaws, especially those in his voice. I had become his confidant.

So I spent many days and nights with Marshal and a video camera. (I had hoped to include those talks in this book, but legal obstruction from Maggie's team would not allow this.) Sometimes visitors stopped by, but we rarely left the hotel room, as Isle found the outside world "distracting" to his progress.

Usually, I'd begin by provoking him. I'd try to make him feel uncomfortable by challenging him with abrasive statements or offensive opinions. I'd pinch him, break a plate, scream and curse until I got some kind of reaction—facial, bodily, olfactory, anything. And if I was successful, in the space of a few minutes I'd watch the transformation begin: his eyes fogging over and then clearing up, his neck muscles tensing and relaxing, the skin on his forehead raising and lowering. His whole self was dipping in and out of awareness like a radio tuning itself to a particular frequency. With each session he became quicker and more efficient. On good days it was among the most remarkable human feats I've ever witnessed: a man living in a constant state of being born and dying, endlessly perfecting himself for the situation he was in.

The following interview is the last of our series of talks in Vegas, and the first of them to be public. We spoke onstage at The Colosseum on a sunny Saturday afternoon in front of a live audience. The event was sold out, and stretched out for fifty minutes longer than expected, mostly due to the extensive question-and-answer period that followed our talk. By the end of the second hour, I was shooting Marshal looks about cutting off the audience's questions, but I could see in his eyes that he was as eager as they were. So we pressed on.

* * *

[audience applause as INTERVIEWER *and* MARSHAL ISLE *take their seats]*

INTERVIEWER: So you're living in a palace now.

MARSHAL ISLE: *[laughs]* Yes, for the next six months, till the residency ends.

I: And you've been involved with this whole project since the beginning, is that right?

MI: Yes, which was about four years ago.

I: And what aspects of the show are you working on?

MI: Everything. Lighting, music, choreography, set list, costume, choosing the crew, diet, schedule. Put 'em all in a pot. Mix it up. Funny thing is, I know nothing about most of this stuff, but even if I can't turn on a light, I do know what effect the light has on the audience—red, yellow, white, bright, soft. And that's all Maggie wants from me. When we started this whole project, all we had in mind was the impression she would make. Not the music. Not the dancing. The impression.

I: And she just put you in charge from the start.

MI: Mm hm.

I: You've joined at a very important time in her career.

MI: The renaissance.

I: Was she ever considering stepping away from music altogether?

MI: She was. Right after the Magdalena years, when she took the turn back toward Maggie. It was a significant moment, both for her and for PM as a whole, because she was returning to her original personality. Back to where she started. It's not easy and not many people have done this. It's a whole different process, and her p was quite drained at that point, so I had to try some new methods. In her case, the process created a kind of self-awareness that prevented her from performing for a few years.

I: Did you help to make that turn?

MI: I did, yeah, at the old soundstage. And a feisty turn it was.

I: So you're to blame for depriving us of Lena's next record?

[audience laughter]

I: And so when she came out of that turn, what was the situation? She just didn't enjoy making music anymore?

MI: Well, coming out of a turn, as I'm sure some of you know, there's a period of hollowness. It's a total lack of any drive. Most guests love this feeling. But there are some who can't handle it. They find it uncomfortable.

I: I've heard it called "feeling skeleton."

MI: Right. It's about working from the inside out, starting deep within the body, where it's dark, where the bones are, and then slowly moving your awareness outward, toward the skin. But to do that, you have to begin at complete ignorance.

I: Is it true that Maggie had to be restrained for the turn?

MI: She was a little wild, yes. I got scratched up, which happens from time to time. It's not a state I encourage, ferocity, but sometimes it's necessary. During that skeleton period, the p has to circulate to all the parts of the body—fingers, toes, interspaces. It's like pins and needles all over. With Maggie, she kept screaming at us to stop hugging her, even though, when you watch the tape, you can clearly see that no one was touching her. She was slapping away someone who wasn't even there. We'd leave the room and she'd keep slapping and screaming, "get her off me."

I: Hallucinating.

MI: But it wasn't that she was *seeing* or *hearing* anything unusual. It was all haptic. She kept saying she *felt* something wrap its arms around her, enter her vagina, her ears, her mouth.

I: Was this because she was returning to Maggie?

MI: We were trying new techniques. We really had to pull new p for this turn. So the fighting, it could've been due to a lot of things. I've seen some of the footage from her previous turns, and she'd always bounce back easily. She'd be onstage in a few days. But this time, it was a very long journey back. Years. Like I said, she wasn't sure she'd ever perform again.

I: How long have you two known each other?

MI: Nine years. She was a guest on the show in '05. During Magdalena.

I: That was right before her hiatus.

MI: We met backstage. Mayah and I were doing some preshow

prep work in our dressing room and one of Mag's assistants knocked and asked if she could join the two of us. Now, normally, at that time, Mayah wouldn't even have *considered* letting anyone in during prework—she was very private about that—but that episode, she knew it would be important for the movement, for the show, and she didn't want to jeopardize the situation, so she invited her in and a friendship was born.

I: When you say jeopardize the situation—

MI: She didn't want Magdalena to cancel or walk off the set, which was a possibility. You know how she was.

I: The great capricious diva.

MI: And we all loved her for it. You need divas in the world. And that day, when she joined us for the work, that's when I really saw the softness of her p. How malleable she kept it. How perfectly superficial and elegant. And all of that, I think, is thanks to her diva nature.

I: To be honest, I'm surprised you're willing to talk about her personalities so freely.

MI: Of course.

I: I just remember the policy with Mayah. No talk of old personalities allowed.

MI: Maggie does things differently. She wants the whole process transparent. No more forgetting. But of course, that's new policy, and you're right, she wasn't always like that. During Lena, she wouldn't talk to anyone she considered bad for her personality. When she was getting ready for a show, no one could speak to her. When she'd make the walk from her green room to the stage, all the other bands would have to stay hidden in their dressing rooms, doors closed, with one of Lena's guards on watch. And after a show, she'd walk directly offstage, slide into her car, and be driven off before anyone could congratulate her. Everyone took it as an elitist thing, but it wasn't. It was just the only way she could keep going. One wrong posture could throw her off for days. And she'd keep extensive notes, recording everything that affected her. Any food or person or sound. She told me once that if she smiled with the wrong muscles, she'd start to picture her face as a "nasty curtain of flesh"—that's how she put it. Horrific, right? What a nightmare it must have been for her. She had to be so careful about everything. She had to be perfect. Because that's why people loved her.

I: I feel like every time I read about the Magdalena tour she was storming off a stage mid-set.

MI: She'd throw fits at every show.

I: And wasn't there some incident at the Grammys? When she dropped the award.

MI: Right, that's right. She got on her knees and sang to the little broken gold gramophone parts. Everyone thought she'd lost her mind.

I: I never saw a Lena show, but I saw Miss in the early '90s in Orange County, when she was still playing to smallish clubs. I remember, she came out and sat down at the piano and started a song but kept hitting wrong notes. It was a little embarrassing. It was like watching someone hurt herself in public. Because it wasn't as if she didn't care. She'd get frustrated, try a different song, and then flub that one too. And then, at some point she started kicking the piano and she stepped down from the stage and started pushing her way through the audience to the back of the club. No spotlight or anything. I'd thought she was leaving but then I started to hear this very muffled, distant voice, and it was her, singing into a mirror on the wall. But again, it wasn't like she was crazy. People kept suggesting she was too high to know what she was doing, which, maybe she was, but I got the sense that she was very aware of what was going on. And it went on for a while. She did quite a few songs like this, a cappella, and then she just walked out the front door and didn't come back. It was—nobody knew what to do. We all stood there for a while, waiting for her to come back in, but she didn't. That was the whole concert.

MI: Love that story. I actually didn't see any of those performances in person, but I've watched a lot of them on video. I've studied every move, every pose, and I've got to say that I think these new performances are more generous than any of those—Miss, Mala, Lena . . . all of them. This is all personalities at once. The queen is back.

I: Has she stopped making turns?

MI: Let me say this: we're always working on her. Every day we're watching rehearsal videos, concert footage, all that. She has a library of her whole career, and we're always studying it, refining it. But it's different now. These days, she's always turning. That's the new path.

I: Newness has always been her thing. Avoiding what she's done before.

MI: "An elegant line never returns."[9]

[audience woots]

---

[9] A lyric from the 1999 single "Unaddicted."

I: Quotes from the master.

MI: For those of you sticking around, you'll hear that one in a few hours. But that's it. That's all I'm going to say about the show. *[laughs]*

I: Or what's that line? "Addicted to the new you." Is that it?

MI: Yes, yes.

I: I often wonder about musicians playing the same songs every night on tour, finding something worthwhile in the same material over and over, for years. But with Maggie, she's always changing the way she plays them. I remember when she did "Consequence" at the Super Bowl in '04—I barely recognized it. The melody was flipped, she made up new words. It almost wasn't the same song.

MI: It's why people bootleg her shows. Always turning. Always turning.

I: That performance was Mala. I'm curious how you would describe her? I've always had trouble grasping what she was going for with that period.

MI: The voice was a big part of it. When she sang, she'd project p from the center of her throat. *[points to his Adam's apple, growls]* She'd tighten her sternocleidomastoids to get a little strain. Not too much. Just enough to get a little p in the cracks.

I: Mala didn't go over very well with critics, which surprised me, since all the other turns have been so mediagenic.

MI: Of course, that whole personality was unattractive. It was supposed to be. The way she dressed with the black, corrugated codpiece.

I: The steel mesh cape.

MI: Plus it was all reactive moves. She built that character on the defensive. She'd send all those little aggressive shudders down her spine. *[shakes his shoulders and hips]*

I: I remember the "Sharpen Up" video. I think every American high school girl slipped those spasms into their dance vocabulary that year.

MI: Remember this one? *[opens and closes both hands in quick flicking motion]* Same kind of move. She could aim the p around her body like that. But that was hard to keep up. She did all that by attacking herself from the inside out. She'd build up an intense fury before shows. She'd sit in a dark closet cultivating it backstage for an hour. There's this rehearsal footage from New Year's where she's teaching that group of ninety-four dancers how to make all those little lurches and jabs, and it's great to watch, because the dancers couldn't really do them. And it's 'cause you have to be pissed. That's the only way they'll work.

I: Would you say Mala was a toxic personality?

MI: I mean—

I: Unless you'd rather not discuss that.

MI: By all means, let's discuss it. *[taps feet]* She was the bad girl. Toward the end of that personality, she wasn't healthy. She wouldn't eat real food. Just sour gummy worms and candy corn all day. And she couldn't sleep for more than a few hours. So that's when she started taking high doses of

Ambien, mixed with various analgesics. And when she overdosed at the Maritime[10] that was an OD on Mala. All that p was too much to hold. It needed expectations. Every personality has to eat something, and Mala, unfortunately, ate ambition.

I: It needed to be praised.

MI: Not praise. That's different. Praise is kinetic energy. It's tangible. Someone says something nice to you, they write something complimentary about you. But expectations are harder to pin down. They're more like potential energy. And she took the turn toward Mala to create those expectations, to have a certain effect on her audience, which is dangerous because the world is fickle. As soon as it stops anticipating your next move, your food supply has run out.

I: Let's change gears here. I want to ask you about the end of *M!* I haven't heard you talk about this much publicly since the final show. Do you think it should have ended when it did? Did it run its course?

MI: Twenty-one seasons. That's a good life.

[audience applause]

I: It's true, but at the same time, did you think there was more to be done with it? Do you think Mull and the trial ended it prematurely?

MI: No, I don't, and here's what I'll say about all of that. This is medicine. Experimental medicine. There are risks. No one has ever claimed that any kind of healing is free of risk,

---

[10] The Maritime Hotel in Manhattan.

right? Drugs, diet, exercise. All these things are fatal if they go wrong. You asked me if Mala was toxic. You used that word. And the answer is, maybe. It's possible. Because all medicine is toxic, depending on the context. What heals one person kills another. If you take just the right amount at the right time under the right circumstances it *will* help you. Or it will hurt you *and* help you. Both. At once.

I: In light of that, maybe we could talk about the comas?

MI: The women in Florida, in Boca [Raton]? Sure. Let's address that, too. First of all, both of them were pushing the safe age for an intensive self-treatment like that. They were what—seventy-seven, seventy-eight?

I: Maybe older.

MI: Maybe older! Now, I think it's great to be engaged with p at that age, but I also think you have to be sensible. P gets weaker. Like everything else in the body. At that age, the best thing to do is work with what you already have. No practitioner I know would have encouraged those women to be making turns.

I: So you think it was largely their fault?

MI: Tsch. Of course it was. *Fault* is a dirty word, of course, but, yes. I always try to instill in people just how powerful the work is. Even if it seems easy when you watch it done on TV. It's not benign. It absorbs you. And at the age of seventy-eight, you need to be putting your p elsewhere, into basic, daily lessons. The gradual turns.

I: Big turns are for the young.

MI: I mean. I could go on and on, because I think there's a lot to be said here about growing old with dignity, but I hope that these incidents, all of them, are testament to the problems of ignoring your age.

I: Right.

MI: I apologize if I seem riled up here.

I: Oh no, I think we all understand. I wanted you to speak your mind on this. Age is a conflicted subject these days.

MI: It should be. I hope everyone here is as sick of ageism as I am.

[audience applause]

I: Speaking of which, we were discussing a story from Maggie's childhood earlier. She hated being a child, it seems like.

MI: Yeah. She felt oppressed.

I: And you were saying how she dropped out of high school—

MI: Yes, there was an incident with a young boy. Long story.

I: Well, I don't know anything about this and I'm sure everyone here would love to hear you tell it.

[audience applause]

MI: Sure. I only know parts of the story, and I'm betting Maggie could do a better job, but I'll try. So, this was when she was in high school, and it began when she met a boy named Tooth. It wasn't his real name, of course, but everyone called him that, I think because he had rotten teeth, and only a few of them. He was poor and lived on the back of the mountain where I guess dental hygiene wasn't great.

I: This was in rural Georgia, where she was raised, right? Blue Ridge Mountains.

MI: That's right. I've never been. From the way Maggie tells it, I get the sense that Tooth lived in a *very* rural place. Not a farm, but a sort of rustic camp. No running water or electricity. And she'd tell me how his shoes and clothes had big holes and . . . you have to hear Maggie do his voice. She puts good p into it. But yeah, he was dirty and as you can imagine he wasn't loved by the other kids. He smelled bad and he'd do stuff like, he'd sneak out to the corner of the yard during recess and shit in his pants and then not wash it out, so it would just stay there, drying to his legs, and the stink would fill up the classroom. That kind of thing. All the children would hold their noses when they walked past him and make barfing sounds.

I: Oh geez.

MI: And Maggie, of course, the little pious angel, even then—she befriended him in class when no one else would. She ate with him. She pretended to laugh at his jokes, even though I guess his speech was difficult for her to understand.

I: Maggie wasn't raised poor, though.

MI: No, she wasn't. And that's important. This area—I think her father had taken a job there, as a scientist—it was a destitute little town, the way she describes it. And also, she was fifteen but Tooth was a little younger. Twelve or so. But at this school everyone was in the same building—older kids, younger kids. It was small. Maggie showed me a picture of her class and there were maybe eight kids in it.

I: So she befriended this boy out of pity.

MI: Well, maybe. She says it was more about him being a kind of blank slate. She could try out different things with him. She could act in different ways and she didn't have to care about being judged. She'd invite him over to her house and perform her ideas for him all afternoon. She was—I don't know if you've seen pictures of her as a young girl, but, you know, there are early glimmers of the loud and proud Maggie we all met in the '80s. And she'd be creating these private performances with costumes and poses for years. There are a few videos of her doing these routines. They're great. She'll be out on the lawn rolling around, swinging from trees, dancing, singing, drumming on everything. But ultimately, she needed an audience. And who better than little Tooth?

I: And I'm sure he just loved that.

MI: So every day she danced and he watched and at some point she started to have some feelings for him, which, if you can just imagine: a future pop star infatuated with this shit-caked little boy living in the hills. And she'd see these kids at school calling him Tooth and making faces at him, and she wanted to help him, because she cared about him. Maybe not romantically, but she cared. So one day, she brought him back to her house and both of them got into her parents' shower and she used an entire bar of soap on every little inch of him. And just—you can imagine the black, awful water that came off him. Feces and dirt and grease, whatever had collected in his hair, bits of coal.

I: But they're in the shower together.

MI: Right, yeah. And nothing sexual happened, or so she says, but something else *did* happen, which is that she felt this vibrating feeling. And she called it "feam."

I: Like in her songs?

MI: Yeah, and it's this term her mom always used, and her grandmother, and it's been passed on. Just as part of her family language. It's hard to explain it exactly. I don't think I fully understand it—but it happens when she can feel someone's p, when she connects with it. Sometimes it's when she physically touches them, but she can also get it from just watching someone from across the room or in a movie.

I: It's like compassion or—

MI: Yeah, but it's more specific than that. She says there isn't really an English translation. It's a certain kind of love, you could say. I mean, at the time, in the shower, she wasn't thinking about p yet. She hadn't even heard of that term, but what she was thinking was *feam.* That made sense to her. It was the only word she had for the feeling. And what's interesting is that now, when she tells this story, she says it's the first time she knew about p. She didn't call it that, but it's the first time she related to that side of herself. Now she feels it all the time, with a lot of people. It's how we chose the crew for the show tonight. It's how she chooses directors for her music videos. It's how she chose me. She always goes by that feeling.

I: Have you felt this? Feam?

MI: Yeah, yeah. So have you, I'm sure. We just don't call it that. Only her family does. It's their family word.

I: And she felt it with Tooth.

MI: Yeah. I think she felt she was doing something just purely good. Helping this boy, wiping him down, turning around the direction of his life. She wanted the kids to stop insulting him. And that was all part of this feam, I think: the feeling that she was doing no wrong. And as she sees it, that feeling, right then, in the shower, it changed her life.

I: It brought her to where she is now.

MI: Exactly. It's what lit the fire. And she's feeling great about herself. She cleans up Tooth, cuts his hair, dresses him in new clothing, and then sends him home. All is good. But a few hours later, there's a banging on her front door. She looks out the window and sees Tooth's father waving around a double-barreled shotgun. And when Maggie opens the door he aims the gun right at her, at this little whiff of a girl, and he says, "If you ever touch my son again, I'll blow off your head." And this is in front of her parents, who have no idea what's going on. They didn't even know who Tooth was because Maggie had been keeping him a secret. And so, then, clearly, they forbid her from seeing this kid again, because they don't want her to get hurt. But does she listen? Hell no. This is a woman who, even now, cannot be reasoned with. So of course she kept eating lunch with him every day, spending all her free time with him, taking him shopping for music, for records, which he had to hide from his parents.

I: A secret affair.

MI: Right, but the way she says it, she wasn't—she couldn't help it. She was infatuated. Again, not in a romantic way, but she just thought about him all the time—how she could *help* him, and, I think she really, earnestly wanted to save him. To culture him. She wasn't really scared by the shotgun thing. She was stimulated, I think. And so eventually, one night, she sneaks out of her house and drove to the community where Tooth lived and she started snooping, asking around for him, knocking on doors, waking up the neighbors, until she finds his house, where his family lived. And it's just a tiny, small, one-room shack in the woods, which for her, was shocking. How depressed it was.

I: She wasn't raised like that.

MI: And no one's home. So she decides to sneak in. She climbs through the window and she starts looking around and she discovers Tooth's wooden chest with all his belongings and she started digging through it. She doesn't even know what she's looking for. She was in a frenzy. She's losing her rational mind over this kid. Because up until then in life, she'd been a straight, obedient daughter. Straight A's. Strong athlete.

I: Lovesickness does that.

MI: For her, it all comes back to feam. It was all she could think about. She just wanted to feel it more and more. She had some kind of rescue fantasy. And when Tooth and his family came home in the morning, they found her, she was—according to them, she had fallen asleep in Tooth's bed, and when they tried to wake her she was in this panicky, manic state. She didn't know where she was, who she was, how she got there. She kept trying to grab at Tooth and embrace him. They didn't know what to do with her. She was an animal.

I: Some kind of a nervous breakdown.

MI: Oh yeah. After this, she had to get counseled. By law, she had to, because Tooth's family had notified the police about her. So it was bad. She stopped going to school, mostly because of the ridicule she got. Everyone knew she'd developed this questionable, criminal obsession with the kid who shit his pants. They called her "stalker." She was totally ostracized.

I: Right, and at that age, acceptance is everything.

MI: But even after all this—leaving school, therapy—she still couldn't stop thinking about him. It kept going! She often says that this obsession is what led to her first turn. She wanted to be past it.

I: Is this what the song "Grady" is based on?

MI: Yeah, yeah.

[audience woots]

I: In a funny way, little Tooth led Maggie to us today.

MI: Yes, he did.

I: So thank you, Tooth!

[audience laughter]

Maybe that's a good point to switch over to some crowd-sourced Q&A?

MI: Let's do it.

I: OK, so how this will work is, anyone who wants to ask a question, we have two microphones at the front of both aisles and you can just queue up behind them. I see a few of you already have. Let's start *[points]* with the young woman in the black dress over here.

AUDIENCE MEMBER 1: Me? Hi Marshal! My name's Patty.

MI: Hi, Patty.

AM1: Wonderful to hear you speak tonight. I'm such a fan.

MI: Thank you.

AM1: Well, for me, I really love Miss Maggie and the whole "Evolve" period. I just—that personality was so important to me and, you know, I think loads of other fans feel the same. There was just something so true about that album and the music was pretty good too, even though it's definitely not my favorite album. But it wasn't about the music for me, really. I fell in love with Miss for the attitude. Her golden ringlets, the Cleopatra eyeliner . . .

MI: Yes.

AM1: And when you have such a good thing going like that, how do you decide to, like, leave it behind? I mean, if I were her, I don't think I could've moved on. I would've wanted to be Miss forever.

MI: I hear you. Essentially, it sounds like you're saying you don't enjoy endings, which I can understand. But endings happen all the time. When someone walks out of a room or ends a phone call.

I: Or exits the stage.

MI: That's what makes a personality good. How it ends. That's how it's preserved, when it becomes real. In some ways, it's the most important part of the whole turn. Say you meet someone at a party. They make an impression on you. You get to know them. They leave. You never see them again. In that case, their exit was the end of that personality for you. The beginning and ending all happened in one night. Their personality is simply whatever happened at that party. Now, with Miss, she just happened to be walking out the door very publicly, in front of the whole world. But she had to leave at some point. If she'd stuck with Miss for the last fifteen years, I think you, Patty, you wouldn't be here right now. It wouldn't have remained attractive to you. Your interest would have waned, because, maybe Miss worked well then, at that time, for you at your age, but now it wouldn't. She was made for the late '90s and she will always be remembered that way because she walked out the door at the precise moment she was no longer relevant.

AM1: Right. I get that.

MI: If you're good—and Maggie is—you can see this moment before it happens. That's the art of personality.

I: I'd say the same of Mayah. She left at the exact right moment.

MI: Talk about art! What a nice, long breath of personality we got from her, right?

[audience applause]

I mean, how much can one personality do? How many people can it affect? And no, I don't think I'd be saying these things right now if she hadn't left when she did, if she'd stuck around just a second more. We all think turning toward the personality is fundamental, but turning away from it is how you become immortal. It isn't a full personality until it's over.

AM1: That's so good. Yes. Thanks. Thank you.

I: Next question over here.

AUDIENCE MEMBER 2: Hi, Mr. Isle. I was just—I heard you say that it's harder for Maggie to make a turn now, compared to before, and—

MI: When did I say that? *[gesturing in circles]*

AM2: Tonight. Earlier.

MI: Oh yeah? Well, it's true.

[audience laughter]

MI: So, yes, the difficulty is that she has a lot of eyes pointed at her now. Her audience has grown and she now has this devoted fan base who follows her every move and glow. For instance, there's this performer, Margo, who does concerts out in Seattle—what are they called?

I: "Impersonalities"?

MI: Right. He has the wigs and outfits and he does this one-man act for about ninety minutes where he dances through Maggie's biography. He's sent her videos of him doing this, along with a sort of spreadsheet he made of all her glows. Any time she was in an advertisement, anytime she did a photo shoot, album cover, live video—he's gone through all the public appearances she's ever made and has very carefully itemized each one. It's impressive. He's named and dated every little glow. All the vocal flips. And he has all these great phrases for them: "Wandering eye on top of high cheekbones," "Bird eating its own feathers," "The inside of a mountain." And he charts all this stuff out for the sake of his performances, which are astonishing. He probably does a better version of "Don't Be" than she did. *[laughs]* Maggie actually agrees. We've both heard him. It's—he's amazing. I love his Lena and his early Maggie stuff is spot on. It's uncanny, seeing him. And that's just one impersonality. There are probably hundreds of these performers all over the world.

I: Super fans.

MI: And of course there are plenty of other people who follow her just as closely who don't impersonate her. But my point is, Maggie is under intense scrutiny from all angles. So many lives are affected by her personality every day. And so, when she designs a turn, she has to take all of these people into consideration. That's her job.

I: You make her sound like a politician.

MI: Well—*[laughs]*

I: You've worked with quite a few public personalities, though. Isn't this the case with all of them?

MI: Sure. But with a singer like Maggie, it's different. Her work is personal, confessional. People are looking to her personality for comfort. She's not an actor. She's always portraying *herself.* And when I say she has a harder time with treatment, this is why. People know far more about Maggie than they do her music. Like *Undying*—the Mae period—most people couldn't hum a single tune off that record, but the posters continue to sell better than any other piece of merch. And it's all because of how she carried herself. This is what people remember. The music was just a soundtrack.

I: It was a vehicle for her personality.

MI: It's all a vehicle—the clothes, the diet plan . . .

AM2: Ooh, if you don't mind me asking, what *is* the new Maggie diet?

MI: It hasn't gone public yet, but we've all been on it for about two years now—everyone on staff. I can't reveal specifics, but one essential, essential aspect of it is the daily sixteen-hour fast, which is something I'd recommend to everyone. You won't lose any weight on it. It's just an extra-long fast from dinner until breakfast. If you eat dinner at 7 p.m., don't eat anything until 11 a.m. That's it. And the point is to *feel* hunger. To experience what the body does when it's hungry. Everyone is scared of being hungry all the time. But we *should* feel hunger. It destabilizes us right. It isn't starvation. It's just enough hunger to get to know your GI tract, to say, "Hello, intestine."

[audience laughter]

I: OK, let's move on to the next question.

AUDIENCE MEMBER 3: So lovely to see you today, Marshal. I've been admiring your work since you first came out. And honestly, I was never really a fan of Maggie until you stepped in. You know, all my girlfriends loved her and I just never got it. And then you came on and it really turned me around. So thank you. But anyway so my question is about all these other hosts who've continued on after you. I'm thinking of, like, Vicki Shore and Dr. Todd—and I'm curious what's your take on them? Because I can't even watch that stuff.

[audience laughter]

MI: Of course, I'm biased, too, but Shore and Todd do right by their guests. They are both doing their part to turn society.

AM3: You like them?

MI: Well, I won't comment on what I think of the shows. That's not relevant.

I: But, just to jump in here—this was Mayah's mission, right? She *wanted* people to pick up where she left off with PM. In fact, I'd say that Maggie, more than any of the other hosts, is currently carrying the torch. Mayah would have loved that.

MI: That's true, for sure. Honestly, she never even liked that term, *PM*. That was the media's invention. She wanted the movement to be folded *into* culture. She wanted personality work to be part of daily life, not segregated into a separate subculture. She wanted a domestic revolution, which is not an implausible idea. Think about romantic relationships in America, how much they've changed their everyday meaning in the last hundred years. It's not that people don't still have partners for their entire lives. Some do. But there's also another fluid approach to dating and marriage and reproduction and romance. People experiment, step into relationships for a few months, a few years, a few decades, and then step out. It wasn't always like that. Romantic relationships are more like how friendships used to be. They can be casual or intense, short or long.

I: And you'd like to see personalities become fluid like that.

MI: Yes, exactly. We could develop a more diverse relationship with them. Some people could maintain the same relationship throughout their life, others could skip through personalities by the week. Mayah wanted to push us toward that freedom. And I think Maggie is also helping to make that happen. And I see Vicki and Mark [Todd] and any other host as helpful in that way, too, even if they give different points of view. Even if I disagree with them. The more these ideas float around, bump into us, sprout new limbs, the better for all of us.

AM3: So, so you don't think that all these other hosts are hurting the ideas Mayah created?

MI: If ideas are so delicate, they're not very valuable, are they? The real idea was to simply create awareness toward p.

I: You think people are more aware now than they were, say, a decade ago?

MI: Ten years ago, PM might have been on the tip of everyone's tongue, on the cover of every magazine, but now it's settled into a quieter awareness, and I think that's ultimately a good thing. It's the same with any cultural transformation. The spectacle happens, it's fun, everyone is excited, but then, when everyone stops looking, that's when the slow, meaningful shifts can start happening.

AM3: Thank you, Marshal. Looking forward to tonight.

I: Next question over here. *[points]*

AUDIENCE MEMBER 4: Hi, Marshal. I'm Jack.

MI: Hey, Jack.

AM4: Hey. So, um, I've always been curious about, did you feel your own personality was affected by the Mull turn? I mean, obviously, it had to be, but your turn was made for the show, right?

MI: You could look at it that way.

AM4: I just mean, you were made to be a part of the movement, right? To fulfill that purpose. But my question is, now that the show is over, wouldn't that personality be over too?

MI: *[laughs]* Should I leave? *[stands and points to the curtain]*

[audience laughs]

AM4: No, I didn't mean—

MI: *[sits]* I understand what you're saying. It's a fair question. But when you use the word *purpose*, I think that's where I lose you. A well-designed turn isn't made for a single purpose. It's loose and pliant. I would never suggest making a turn toward a job or a partner or a political office, really. Because once that relationship ends, or the job changes, as it will, then where's your personality? It's purposeless. Maggie doesn't make a turn toward her career, toward success. She makes it for the love of p. You see politicians who shape themselves for approval. They look terrible.

[audience laughter]

And yes, I've considered a new p, and I have a little journal where I write my designs, but I don't think I'm quite ready yet. We'll see.

I: I was wondering this earlier, so I'm just going to ask now: I want to take a quick read of the room. How many people here have taken a turn?

[approximately 300–400 hands go up, about a fifth of the audience]

And how many of you have held on to it?

[a few hands go down, most stay up]

MI: Oh, that's nice to see. And how many of those were made by Mayah?

[most hands go down, fewer than ten remain]

WOMAN'S VOICE FROM THE BACK: Hi Marshal, honey!

MI: Who is that?

[woman stands; a spotlight moves to her]

Is that Dinah? My god, look at that! Come on up here, Dinah. I can't see you back there, hiding in the shadows.

[Dinah approaches stage; audience applauds]

I: Look at this reunion. When did you two last see each other?

MI: I think . . .

DINAH RAND: It was before the final season in '06. You came out to the house for a checkup.

MI: Oh, yes.

DR: I remember, we spoke for a few hours alone and then the

camera crew arrived. We did a storytelling segment and I made you your first Arnold Palmer.

MI: I remember. A good first. Just iced tea and lemonade.

I: Dinah, when was your turn?

DR: Uh, '98. In the fall. October.

I: So it was a soft turn. Before Marshal's time.

DR: Oh yeah, long before, but he and I have got to know each other over the years, haven't we?

MI: Oh yeah. Mayah always talked about your personality with everyone. As if it was the golden moment of the early years.

DR: That's sweet. What wonderful work that woman did. And my family—they couldn't have been more grateful, either. They're actually here, up in the balcony there. *[gestures to the back of the room]*

I: How have you been doing with Dinah since you two last saw each other?

DR: I feel like—it's hard to say, but I do think it's blurred a little. I mean, listen, to be totally honest, I stopped my vocal stretches. I did. And sometimes, now, I'll be talking and I'll hear Dana come out—I'll hear that husky tone cracking out of my throat and all those nasty words spilling out of me. I hate it. And of course I know how to make her go away, but I don't always do it. You know, with Dana, she was visual. She was vain. And all her anxiety came from that. And sometimes I still obsess about myself, and how I look to other people, and I can feel that same numb hand thing Dana would get at parties.

MI: Do you miss her?

DR: No. Never ever. But I also haven't been stopping myself from letting a little of her come in.

MI: You shouldn't have to be trying so hard.

DR: I know. I know. You say that, but still I do. I try. Like a boob.

MI: When is this happening?

DR: It's the worst when I wake up, for sure. I can really feel her then. I picture her as a mist that floats in the room at night, hanging over my bed, and as soon as I fall asleep, she drizzles down and works her way into me all night long. It gives me the creepies to think about. But, um, am I sounding gloomy? I don't mean to. I'm doing good. I'm happy with my choice. I'm grumbling, but I'm doing great in life. To be honest, I came here so I could get a little shot of inspiration back into me. So I could get back on my five-by-fives. 'Cause sometimes I forget how much I want a clean personality, how good it is for me. A lot of my friends back home aren't into the movement, you know? So it's hard to find support. But I really believe that if you don't have the right p you don't have anything. And I never *ever* felt like Dana was right. She was just a mess. I mean, I never had that "real me" feeling with her. But, anyway, I don't want to gab on and on. I'm glad I came and that we got to talk a bit. So lovely to see you.

MI: You too. See you at the show tonight.

DR: You sure will.

I: *[points to AM5]* Over here. The man in the suede jacket.

AUDIENCE MEMBER 5: Hello. First of all, this has been a great talk. My wife, Sara, brought me here. She's a huge Maggie fan. And I admit, I've never seen a full episode of *M!* I've heard all about it from Sar, but . . . I don't know, I guess it never interested me—the whole fucking-with-your-personality thing, pardon my language. It felt culty. But I can admit when I'm wrong, and what you've been saying here actually makes a lot of sense to me, the way you talk about it. Except, the part I don't like is being so public about it. I don't want to be on television. I don't want my personality being written about. I hate that shit. I'd just want to be private, at home.

MI: Well, first of all, you're right. The show catered to the public. We wanted to reach people. That was the point.

AM5: Yeah, I'm not like that.

MI: Mayah favored a certain kind of public personality. She loved the energy of that big p. She loved Maggie, for instance. She saw all the turns she made as great performances. *[in Mayah's voice]* "Artworks like that shouldn't be kept from the world!" But it's funny you mention this because, during season 20, we'd been working on a practice that could be done privately, at home. A full turn, at home, done safely. A swapping. We just didn't get a chance to finish it. Maybe one day.

AM5: Could you recommend any private practitioners?

MI: I can't—I really shouldn't give names here, but there are probably a few in this room . . .

[a few woots from the audience]

And most of these practitioners are working out of their homes, one-on-one. They'll have a bodywork table, a stress reader, maybe some kind of proprietary tonic. It's usually an intimate experience. They're not working with isolation tanks like we did on the show, and it's not the fully loaded situation that Maggie does, with a dozen specialists watching her, three people rubbing out her glows at once. But then again, it's a different kind of personality they're producing, private practitioners. It's simpler and probably more suited for daily life.

AM5: Would you, at any point, consider opening your own private practice?

MI: One day, yeah. I'd have to pick a good spot. Some communities—they're not as open to the movement as you might think. I've heard of a few practices being shut down in towns that clearly did not want them. I mean, try and practice within half a mile of a serious lifestyle religion. There's still plenty of that hatred toward us, toward me.

I: They think you're unhinging the soul.

MI: Which, honestly, I don't think that's such a wild accusation. I mean, I even like that phrase you just used—"unhinging the soul." Sure, I'd do that.

[audience laughter]

But yes, one day, in a city that's right, I'd open a little practice, focus on local turns. Essentially, the opposite of what I'm doing now.

I: Affecting millions of people.

MI: And I love it. But I can imagine a small practice being gratifying in a different kind of way. So yeah, I think you should experiment with a few private practitioners, but unfortunately I can't be one of them. Not yet at least.

I: Next question, over here.

AUDIENCE MEMBER 6: Hi, me? Oh, great. Hi, I'm not actually sure I even have a question, I just wanted to show Marshal something and see if maybe, if he had anything to say about it.

MI: Yeah, let's see it.

AM6: *[takes off her sandal]* OK, so just to give my little preamble, when I was fifteen, I was walking on the boardwalk by the beach in North Carolina, and my foot went through a rotten plank of wood. It was pretty traumatic and I couldn't move at first. I had to be dragged out by a few strangers. And when I got out, the whole thigh was torn up and I'd pulled a muscle. And a toe was sprained. The actual injury wasn't too debilitating or anything, though. It hurt, but it wasn't terrible. Even so, it really bothered me. And even when it healed and the pain went away, my concern for the foot didn't. Does that make sense? Like, any time I'd go for a walk, the foot started freaking out. Even just when I'm walking on the sidewalk. It's not pain, exactly. But that feeling, it's always there, like something's wrong with it. It never goes away. And I—I've been to a hundred doctors to check out the foot. And they ran the whole battery of tests and of course, nothing. It's all in my head! I know I'm not delusional. I'd heard your thoughts about your "Broken Leg Personality" and thought maybe that was me. But I'm open to anything. I must have swallowed a million pills over the last ten years to stop thinking this way. I even tried a turn a few years ago, with Dr. Jan Rafael, but it didn't take. I really, really, really wanted it to—and I love what the movement does for people, but I think I'm resistant to it or something.

MI: What happened when you tried?

AM6: Diarrhea. For days. And my emotions were all out of whack for a week after. I'd be laughing and crying all the time. It was awful, especially for my husband.

MI: OK. Let's try something here. Would you be open to that?

AM6: Anything.

MI: Just a quick thing. To start, I want you to tense your face. Put all your tension into it . . . Create a little pocket of p.

AM6: *[visibly tenses]*

MI: Yes, that's good. Maybe even a little more.

AM6: *[tenses more]*

MI: Good . . . Now I want you to move it around. Feel it moving to every part of the face. The eyes and cheeks. The forehead. And just let that dance around your face. Throw the p back and forth beetween your eyes and lips . . . Back and forth . . . Back and forth . . . *[pause]* Now just relax . . . *[pause]* Now again, I want you to tense. But this time focus on pursing your lips . . . *[pause]* That's good. Now again . . . relax . . . Shake it out.

AM6: *[shakes]*

MI: That just keeps it all moving. So now I'm going to give you a series of situations and you're just going to reach for them with the face and with the body. You can close your eyes or you can leave them open. Whatever works for you.

AM6: Sure, yeah.

MI: Come up a little closer toward the stage so everyone can see you.

AM6: *[approaches the stage, closes eyes]*

MI: Ready?

AM6: *[off mic]* Ready.

MI: You're walking through a cutlery store, down a long, narrow aisle. You can see glistening, sharpened knives hanging on every shelf. Ahead of you, another woman is perusing some large chopping blades. You can't see her face, but she is pulling the knives from the shelf, testing their weight, slicing at the air as if cutting invisible fruit. And you can see from the way she holds the blade, the angle of it, the way her torso is in mid-twist, the quick careless pace at which she wields the blade, that it will collide with you if you continue to walk toward her at the rate at which you are now walking. The blade will be driven directly into your eye. But even though you can anticipate this, you find that you are still walking forward. You are compelled forward. Closer and closer.

AM6: *[walks in place]*

MI: And then, here it comes . . . slice!

AM6: *[darts to the side, crouching]*

MI: Good. OK. You moved from the gut. That's important.

AM6: *[opens her eyes]* Yeah?

MI: Now a few quick ones. Someone slaps you.

AM6: *[throws back head]*

MI: You step into a cold shower.

AM6: *[brings hands and feet close to her body]*

MI: A hot one.

AM6: *[spreads open arms, slides hands down her face and chest]*

MI: Your hair's on fire!

AM6: *[slaps her head]*

MI: Your favorite meal is placed before you.

AM6: *[smiles and opens arms]*

MI: Too much.

[audience laughter]

Your hands are chapped by the wind.

AM6: *[spreads fingers]*

MI: Your child isn't your child.

AM6: *[grips her hair]*

MI: OK, that's good. That's just a quick set. Normally, for this kind of prep work for this kind of chronic experience, I'd go through a hundred rounds with you for several hours, but I don't think this is the right place for that. And, obviously, I'd like to work more with you to say for sure, but, from just that little test, I can see that you're dumping all your p into the right side of your body, which is something you can start paying close attention to.

AM6: Oh. I will. Thank you for your help.

MI: Sure, of course. I hope it doesn't cause any diarrhea.

[audience laughter]

MI: You know, as I'm telling you all this, it occurs to me that one of the best examples of this kind of healing from mysterious conditions is sitting right next to me. *[turns to I]* Any insights on all this?

I: Uh, well—yes. Chronic illness made me who I am today. Certainly that's true. But I'm not sure I feel comfortable giving advice . . .

MI: OK, then I'll talk for you. *[laughs]* This personality right here, our fine interviewer—you have truly *become* your condition. In the last decade, I've watched you get to know a whole saga of pains, maladies, and disorders, and what you've learned to do with them is remarkable. You never accept them simply as pain. You direct these feelings into your personality and learn from them. You never *separated* yourself from them. You turn toward your condition, *toward* your problems, because you knew that was the only way you could exist with them. Which I'd say is largely because you didn't find a solution for your problems. Not from any healer. Not even in the movement. Would you say that's right?

I: Something like that.

MI: And for me, observing you go through this—it's been edifying. You've taught me so much—

I: All right, I'll just step in right here and say that, despite how generous you're being, I'm only where I'm at because of you. *[turns to audience]* I know he likes to say how everyone makes their own turns, and that he doesn't do anything, but it's not true. I think we all owe a lot to him.

[audience applause]

MI: Thank you. Could I get you to talk about the disturbance you mentioned earlier?

I: Sure. So it's in my vestibular system, the feeling. It's not quite vertigo but it's a similar condition that no one seems to have a name for. To describe it, this feeling, when it comes, it's like my brain is flapping around in my head and the ground is rushing up at my face. I immediately get nauseous, overwhelmed, and generally miserable. I feel like I'm holding on for dear life, even when I'm standing completely still. Sometimes I'd be clinging to anything or anyone around me. The wall. A chair. Your arm. It's panicky and intense and at first I hated it. I'd spend all day with my face in a pillow, or I'd drink twenty kava shakes to calm me down, but the feeling wouldn't go away. Because all I was doing was trying to escape. I wasn't listening to what the feeling was telling me.

MI: Yes, yes.

I: And so what I eventually had to do, to cope, was to reimagine myself. Because whatever I was doing wasn't helping long term. I couldn't stick my head in the couch and drink kava all day. I was essentially confined to my house. So to get better, I started to get to know the feeling. I'd ask myself, what if this feeling is the only thing I ever knew? My entire life. What if I stopped comparing this feeling to what I considered *normal*, or stable, and just acted like this was perfect reality. As if I were born this way. Obviously, it required a lot of concentration to earnestly consider this question. But I had to. I had to. So what I'd do is, even when I was feeling lightheaded, I'd keep my whole self fully engaged with whatever it was I was doing. I'd cook or I'd take a walk or go buy a lemon. Anything active. The simpler, the better, because I'd have to know that this was my first and only time doing this activity. I was a child again.

MI: Describe what that looks like.

I: Oh, stumbling around, making an ass of myself, grabbing on to people's legs. Usually I'd fail at whatever the task was—I'd drop the lemon—but then I'd do it again, and I'd try to lean down and pick up the lemon as casually as possible. And if that seemed unbearable, I'd know that I was doing it wrong. This wasn't my way of picking up the lemon. This was some other way. Maybe my old way or someone else's way, or the supposed normal way, but it wasn't right for me now, with my head in this state. If I really made a relationship with the feeling, it would *show* me how to pick up the lemon.

MI: And it did.

I: Eventually. But I had to do it every day all the time, with so, so many activities. Going to the bathroom. Talking on the phone. Typing. Drinking water. Listening to music. Driving. Blinking. And the thing is, I can be aware of it right now if I want to. I can focus on the wobble. I just usually don't want to. I've just accepted it, and identified myself with it. To the point where I don't even talk to myself about it much anymore. That feeling *has become* me. It's like Marshal said, I don't separate myself from it. And I bet if that feeling were to immediately drop away, I'd actually feel uncomfortable, like something were missing. I wouldn't feel like me.

MI: Right, this is what I was saying, you've become your condition.

I: I hope so. But, uh, let's move to the next question and stop talking about me. *[laughs]* We're running low on time. Maybe this should be the last one? Over here.

AUDIENCE MEMBER 7: Hi. I just wanted to ask, how is Mull these days? I'm always so curious about her, but there's never any news or updates anymore. Do you think she's been forgotten?

MI: People ask me this a lot, but it's funny, I don't think Mull cares about being remembered or discussed. I think she'd rather be forgotten by the mass public. It's healthier for all of us.

AM7: Do you still see her?

MI: Of course. While I'm staying here in Vegas, I see her a few times a month.

AM7: But you don't want to tell us where she is.

MI: Tell a room of thousands of people? No, I don't think so. But that's not because Mull can't handle visitors. I just think people would go to her for the wrong reasons.

I: Because they want to see Mayah.

MI: Right. Which is not fair to her. It's not her fault people haven't caught up with her. And it's not everyone. It's all those obsessives out there who are demanding the big return of Mayah—that's the problem. We've had some movers come from across the world to see her. And they're loaded up with questions for her, or they have chronic pain they want cured, but after a few minutes, it's clear they're looking for Mayah, not Mull.

I: Mayah hasn't been forgotten, even if Mull wants to be.

MI: Mayah will never be truly gone. She made herself that way. She wanted nothing more than to pass her personality along.

AM7: I also wanted to ask, and I don't mean to be crude, but she doesn't—she's not a, you know, with her diet . . .

MI: She's not eating children, no.

AM7: Just because I saw those photos online—

MI: Polly is the little girl in the photo. She and Mull play together all the time. Usually after school in the yard. She's a friend of hers in the neighborhood. And that whole scenario, with the chasing and the biting—it's one of their games. The photo was taken way out of context.

AM7: But the girl looks so terrified.

MI: Children get excited. They scream like they mean it. They're intense little actors. We're all actors when we're kids, experimenting with our emotions all day long. And I don't know how that photo surfaced, but it's really been taken out of context. Taken at the right moment, at the right angle it could tell any story.

AM7: I guess so.

MI: You seem like you want to believe this.

AM7: No, no! But the blood—

MI: Listen, I don't need to dispel the idea. I think it's an entertaining rumor.

AM7: She doesn't know about it?

MI: Hey. "Mull don't know."[11]

[audience laughter]

But no, she's utterly in the dark about it. That's how she wants to be.

AM7: Is she happy?

MI: Always.

AM7: That's great to hear. I've always been a Mull supporter. Thanks for speaking today.

I: *[whispers off microphone to* MI*, then addresses audience]* OK, looks like I lied. We have time for one more question, and then Marshal needs to head backstage and prepare for the show tonight. Um . . . how about over here. The woman with the topknot.

AUDIENCE MEMBER 8: Oh, good, good. Hi, Marshal. I love your work with Maggie. I've already seen the show a few times and I'm coming again tonight. So, I just wanted to know what you're up to after the residency is over. Will you still be working with Maggie?

---

[11] A popular idiomatic phrase in 2010.

MI: Yes, I'm glad someone asked this. I've been helping Maggie set up some new TTT programs throughout the country. Do all of you know about these?

[mild audience applause]

Not many, it sounds like . . . OK, so TTT is the Time Toward Turning program. It's a new series of sessions for children. We have them set up in five cities already: San Francisco, Los Angeles, Seattle, Paris, and New York. But the idea is to get them in fifty cities by the end of the decade.

AM8: What ages? I have two little boys.

MI: We've worked with them as late as fifteen, as early as two.

AM8: Wow, two? What are you working on at that age?

MI: Motor skills. Everything is in the movement at that age. The sessions are just helping them to get in touch with what little p they can feel.

AM8: You're teaching them how to move better?

MI: We never really teach, not the way you think of teaching. At that age it's all in the watching. It's how you watch that's important. Just giving attention, having your eyes on them. Toddlers are little celebrities. They just want to feel your eyes.

AM8: So true.

MI: We grow out of celebrity. Every child is a star. Just like every child is an actor and an artist.

I: So what age do you start actually teaching, would you say?

MI: Once we start to see a little p in their moves. Usually it's in the bend of their knees or the rotation of the shoulder. Whenever that happens, the lessons begin.

I: Are these programs in schools at all?

MI: Oh, no. Keep us away from schools. *[laughs]* We set up our studios in the parts of cities where there are no schools. We'll get charter buses, drive the students over after school, whatever we can do, but it's important to keep the distance clear to the students. TTT has nothing to do with school. Maggie loves children and she doesn't want them to go through what she went through.

[audience applause]

I: What time is it?

MI: Late.

AUDIENCE MEMBER: 5:30!

I: We should stop. You'll be back on this stage in a few hours.

MI: Actually, I have to get the dancers ready in fifteen minutes.

I: Oh wow. Well, thanks for letting us cut into your prep time. And *[gestures to audience]* thank you all for coming.

[audience applause]

MI: Did I answer all your questions?

[audience applause grows]

Good to hear. Now get ready for the real show.

Afterword

Reading over twenty years of interviews, I find it impossible to sympathize with the young writer asking all the questions. Despite all my personal development, the only thing I see in every transcribed word is my intoxication with the hope of being unique. No amount of editing seems to scrub this away. And yet here I am publishing it anyway, hoping these words might give a little nudge to the turn of culture.

I wrote this book to become a different person. I didn't hate myself. I wasn't unhappy with my life. But I was undoubtedly making myself sick. I just wanted to be me so badly. I loved the possibility of my personality. I believed in it. But thankfully, I believed in Masha, Marshal, Mayah, and Mull more.

It may have taken two decades, but I finally unlearned the prejudice of identity. It's an insight I hope the next generation can benefit from. They'll probably scoff at my inner struggle, just as I do when I look at my parents' confusion toward gender, my grandparents' uneasy relationship with race, and my great-grandparents' medieval views on sexuality. How could they have believed in such flawed myths of their time?

So I ask myself, what myths do I believe now? Do I believe, as many people do, that Marshal is still alive, somewhere deep in the woods, cowering from society's judgment? Do I believe he followed in Mull's footsteps and whittled his personality down to a smooth nub, and hid away in an off-the-grid hut? Or that a renegade personality has possessed him, wiped his memory, and left him unaware of the world he has left behind?

All these stories contain a kernel of faith that Marshal continues to exist, not necessarily as he was, but in some other, hopeful form. I do believe in that kernel. And I believe in believing in the kernel. Rumors are good for us.

Marshal was a masterwork, and he will find a place alongside the great personalities of history: Napoleon, Casanova, Genghis Khan. Like them, he has imprinted himself on all our minds. It's what he was made to do, and he did it without the flash and violence that have always been required of the word *personality*. He made his way into us with ease. I have Marshal in me, and now, after reading this book, so do you. In fact, if you ask a mover like me, Marshal is circulating through every single one of us right now, even if you've never heard his name, even if you've never experienced p.

How could I *not* believe this? I watched a man liquefy his personality and move it like a river. Maybe he'd settle into something for a few minutes, but then, before you could recognize it, he'd be flowing again, so gradually that you wouldn't even notice. Every so often, you'd see Marshal drift by in the squint of his eye, or hear it in the crack of his laugh. He hadn't forgotten that personality, but he also didn't seem particularly interested when it came around. He just waved it on through.

Here was a man having asexual intercourse with himself forever. The days of hard turns were over. The work was over.

Personally, I know I will never reach that level of my practice, but of course that wasn't ever my goal. I just wanted to feel better, and I did that, at least for the most part. Whether or not PM fully healed me, I can't say with any kind of empirical accuracy. All that matters to me now is, I needed a change and I found it in my place and time—the era of the Isle family.

If I'm being honest, I never use my PM techniques anymore. I don't keep up with my five-by-fives, and the movement just isn't on my mind in the same daily way. People don't talk about it like they used to. Mull's tucked away in some soft, silent corner of the world, and I rarely encounter another mover in the city. I hear there's a semi-thriving enclave in Warwick, New York, and once in a while I'll see a poster for a community center program staging a PM interview, but I can't be around a bunch of nostalgic middle-agers reenacting their glory days. That's just not how I want to remember the movement.

The truth is, PM was a trend. For a few years, its ideas rushed through many individuals all across the world and it flourished. It rose, fell, and has faded from the front page of history. But does this make it less valuable? I don't see why. It helped thousands. Trends ebb like waves, pass like storms, as natural as can be. Why must every idea persist? Why does a flash in the pan have less worth than an age-old tradition? If believers knew their religion would lose its influence within a few years, would they stop having faith? No, if knowledge has worth to someone in only a single moment, it still has worth. The notion that every good philosophy must live on forever to be successful is absurd. It's just another tiresome manifestation of our fear of death. The reality is, people die and so should their ideas.

But what about personalities? Can these be immortal? Skin rots and thoughts fade, but what about the soul? Every culture has their ghosts, their disembodied spirits, their lost souls. And what is soul if not an old-timey word for personality?

In my opinion, PM was too complex to survive in this contemporary world. In the hands of the media, a vast system of thought such as this can never be addressed on its own terms. It didn't have enough hard boundaries and direct answers to get snappy headlines, so they reduced it to a name: Isle. I did this, too. Even though we all know the problems of human-on-human devotion, we can't help ourselves. We remain perpetually in love with the myth of a savior, and every year we pick a new one just so we can watch him fail.

There was a moment, after the show ended, when the press declared Isle the most dreaded of celebrity insults: a "has been." But to my surprise, Isle accepted it with gusto. He knew how fickle culture could be, and the challenge of negative criticism seemed only to fortify him. Gossip was his food. He was hungry for any morsels of praise or blame flung at him. He didn't want perpetual admiration. He wasn't a statue, biceps permanently flexed, lips fixed in a grin. He wanted to adapt and turn with the seasons, molding to the capricious shape of the world around him.

This is why Marshal will be forever relevant. As trends wax and wane, and as public opinions sway, he will persist. Not because he's divine or timeless, but because his personality thrives in the face of newness. It sympathetically vibrates with it. Most of us spend our lives sharpening our selves into fine-pointed tools, aimed at a single, specialized goal, but Isle was the great generalist. He opened his self up like a funnel so that all of us could pour through him. While most celebrities dehumanize themselves, simplifying their personas into an archetype, a catchphrase, a manifesto, Isle simply lifted his sensory channels and became sensitive to everything.

Here's another thing I believe: Isle could fall in love with anyone at any time. We've all heard this before. Another ridiculous claim from another crazy mover. But I can say that I personally felt this love and that I've spoken to others who felt it too. I know this idea scares some people, but let me say, Isle couldn't make *you* love *him*—he could only *encourage* it. I saw him do this many times. He looked into you—not *at* you—and found any tiny seed of admiration you had for him and pointed all of his charm at it until it bloomed into love. And he did it invisibly, the way that only a magician could. Maybe in less virtuous hands, this kind of behavior would feel like manipulation; with Isle, it was the work of a healer.

But, of course, that was the *old* Isle. By the end, he'd lost interest in that kind of effort. As time went on, he just wanted to protect his p, not expend it. The last time I saw him, neither of us fell in love. This was in the autumn, and I was living in Manhattan. Marshal had come to town for a private session for an emir. He rarely did this kind of work anymore. Maybe it was a favor. Maybe he needed the money. I don't know. But from what I understood, the final sessions were nothing more than simple conversations.

He wrote me and explained that he had been involved in a year-long search for his birth mother, the woman Masha had called Mimo. He was hopeful that my early interviews with Masha (which I had long since told him about) might contain a few clues to her identity and whereabouts. He didn't want to read them, he said, but asked if I would go through the talks, pull out any relevant material, and then discuss it with him over lunch.

So we met in Tribeca at an experimental gastronomy spot with only two tables and three employees. When I arrived, Marshal was rocking gently back and forth in his chair, as if massaging himself. His face had developed a sunny yellow hue, and he told me he'd been rubbing barberry and probiotics on his face, which he said brighten his skin naturally.

We were served food without ordering: a selection of organ meats including kidneys, sweetbreads, and brains, plus two cups of a root vegetable puree with fermented lemons and fresh dill. Isle ate almost none of it. He was requiring less food than ever before, he said, and was preparing for a "comprehensive water fast" that he hoped would calm a tricky candida infection.

We talked about an offer he had received to host a new personality show, but he seemed uninterested in the topic so I brought out my pad with some of the notes I'd written down about Mimo. I read them aloud, but he seemed equally bored by this topic. So I let him steer the conversation, and pretty soon we were discussing a young man with whom he'd been corresponding for the last few months: Kyle Collier, a name I'd never heard until that day.

Marshal called him a clairvoyant. He'd become fascinated by the boy's drawings and letters, which described parallel worlds where Collier claimed to travel via astral projection. Every night, the boy said his soul left his body and danced through the celestial realm. Supposedly Marshal played some role in these narratives, each one filled with past lives and premonitions and acts of mythical bestiality. Collier would appear as a monstrous, deformed wizard, able to transform other people with his spells. Wild, fantastical stuff.

But according to Marshal, several of the boy's predictions involving himself had been accurate, including the identification of a benign tumor in his left lung. Marshal told me that Collier had "the kind of intuition that needs to be cultivated."

I found it all worrisome, and a few minutes into the conversation I'd firmly decided that Collier was an unhealthy sociopath. But I could see that Isle didn't agree with me. He had some kind of faith in the boy, and talked about him in that dreamy way that suggested he hadn't even considered being fearful. It's a quality I always respected in him, his ability to see the best in people, and so, out of respect and admiration, I suppressed my concern. I finished my meal, nodding and smiling, trying to not upset Marshal's new excitement with my cynical naysaying. It was a cowardly approach that will probably haunt me until the day I die.

A few months ago, the producer of *In View* (the debate show I currently host on PBS) asked me to interview Collier from prison. For obvious reasons, I felt uncomfortable about the assignment, but then I thought, *Who better to do it?* So I agreed, but I said I would rather speak with Collier's family than the boy himself. I wanted to unlearn my idea of the boy as a deranged predator and to instead know him through those who loved him.

Through Collier's mother, I learned that he had been enduring a slow, quiet nervous breakdown years before connecting with Isle. He'd identified as a psychic since he was a small child, and had moved to Las Vegas at the age of twenty-four with the intention of turning his gift into a stage-ready show. His sister said the move was "uncharacteristic and abrupt" for her brother, but hoped it would serve as "a fresh start."

But the transition was challenging for the boy. He failed to establish his divinatory coaching business. He acquired only two clients, and spent all of his savings buying scalped tickets to Maggie's sold-out shows. He stopped speaking to his family and began to stay inside his apartment for weeks at a time, eating only white rice and clear broth. The day he cracked open Isle's chest with a chunk of granite was his twenty-fifth birthday.

This death wasn't an act of menace. Collier adored Isle. He didn't want to hurt him, and to this day he remains convinced that he didn't. To him, the man claiming to be Isle those last few years, the one working with Maggie, who had emerged from a long sabbatical from the public—this was an imposter.

In his notebooks, Collier expressed his hypothesis repeatedly. He diagrammed it in proofs and arboreal-looking charts. At Maggie's concerts, he closely studied any instance of Marshal's onstage movements and marked every inconsistency. He wrote stories about a "double" locking Marshal away and stealing his true self. As Collier saw it, he wasn't murdering his hero, but emancipating him. And when the police found the boy mumbling over Isle's body, whispering about a "pathogen," it's fully clear to me that he wasn't referring to Isle at all—as most reporters assumed—but to his captor.

None of this would surprise Marshal. As I've read over their exchanges, I've come to understand that he agreed with Collier's assessment of him. He hadn't felt right for a long time, and this boy seemed to understand why. Isle nurtured Collier's fantasies, praising the boy for his insight, even in the face of his most radical theories. He seemed relieved by their relationship, and in a way, knowing this has relieved me too.

Or maybe I've just heard the nasty version enough: Marshal was a product of culture and when culture had used him up, it threw him out. No, I was sick of that. By the time Isle died, that kind of storytelling didn't suit me anymore. I wanted to talk about the many ways in which this death was *not* a tragedy. Here was a man who had lived a vast spectrum of lives within the space of a single lifespan. He lived more, felt more, experienced more life than even the oldest living human. So what need was there for despair?

But despite these explanations, I was still heartbroken. I couldn't change that. So I did what we all did. I dragged myself out of bed on a cold winter afternoon, combed my hair, made myself presentable, and attended the memorial service in Bryant Park. I hadn't planned on going, but I couldn't seem to stop myself either. I had a craving that could only be satisfied by mass commiseration.

For three hours I wandered through a field of tearful fans, trying to let go of my grief. Speeches, songs, candles. Vendors selling cheap memorabilia. Maybe it wasn't the glamorous service at La Brea Tar Pits, or the great parade through Golden Gate Park, but sitting on my blanket in the center of Manhattan, I am certain that I felt the presence of Isle, and he was as healthy and alive as the rest of us.